THE FROSTY TASTE OF SCANDAL

CEECEE JAMES

For my Family-333 <3

CONTENTS

BLURB

Elise Pepper has had dates ruined by cold-hearted men before, but she's never had one quite this cold. Cold, as in dead.

Instead of an evening of flirting and ice skating, Elise discovers the dead body of Mr. Hamilton, a mortgage broker with a reputation for shady deals...also known as the Ice-man. Apparently, the murderer had a sense of humor. Or irony.

When Elise's co-worker Sue turns out to be related to the dead man, Elise knows she has to help find the murderer. Between a freak power outage will and a seemingly endless list of people who had good reason to want him dead, Elise has more leads than she can follow. Even the King and Queen of the high school Winter Ball are under suspicion!

With the killer hiding in plain sight, Elise can't narrow down the suspects... this may be her first case where the killer gets away.

CHAPTER 1

*I*t was seven o'clock on a cold December night, not a particularly interesting hour of the day. It was the time just after dinner, but before the snacks and prime time TV. Too late for most projects, but too early to go to bed.

Elise found herself staring down a man standing next to the ice-skate rental counter. The man appeared to be in his mid-to-late thirties with a thin mustache—the type that enticed a giggle at first sight—and stringy brown hair brushed to the side. He was larger than average, both in height and weight, with a brown sweater vest stretched over a belly that more than one person would blame on alcohol indulgence.

He didn't say anything, just continued to stare over the top of his glasses, soda in hand, while the teen behind the counter passed over the skates. His small brown eyes were clear as he glared at her.

Elise took the skates with great apprehension and thanked the teen. She glanced at the man again. What had she done to get on his bad side? She'd only asked the kid for a size seven.

She slipped her boots off and then passed over, her first cute pair in two years. The last six months she'd been a receptionist at the StraightenUp Chiropractic Clinic, a job that actually paid more than minimum wage. She loved the work, and she loved finally having a little breathing room when it came to bill-paying time. Her new boots were topped with puffy fur, and they hugged her feet while still looking adorable.

Unlike these skates.

Elise turned the pair over in her hands as she walked to the nearest bench. The paint was worn off the seat of the metal bench from the thousands of people who'd sat there to lace their skates up. The skating rink was well over thirty years old. Elise imagined even her parents had been there a few times on a date.

A date. That's what Elise was on. She sighed as she tightened the worn laces. Brad had texted just as she arrived to say that he would be late, and he was *so* sorry.

But he was on a case, and she understood.

Well, sort of.

She was still a little disappointed, in a petulant thirty-something-acting-like-a-teen-because-this-was-their-first-date-alone-in-two-months type of way. But still understanding.

The problem was that Elise hadn't been out on the ice since she was a teenager. Since she and Lavina, her best friend, had ruled the ice together with all of their friends, screaming with laughter, cheesy music, and lots of flirting in the darker corners of the rink.

Now, twenty odd years later, it was safe to say apprehension was building. She hadn't exactly grown more graceful through the years. She hoped it was like riding a bike, something you never forgot.

With a deep breath, she stood up on the skates and tottered to the ice. It was now or never. She pulled her gloves on and stepped out onto the ice.

It was just a fluke that her left foot headed to the right and the right to the left. At least, that's what she told herself as she scrambled to reach for the wall.

A group of teens skated by, laughing. Elise was sure it was about her. If she was a teen, she'd laugh at the goofy old lady, too.

To add insult to injury, as she slowly looked around, she confirmed that she was the oldest person here.

Probably by double.

Elise cautiously let go of the wall and pushed herself forward. *Left, Right. Left. Right.* Her smile grew as she glided on the ice. But what fresh news was this? She suddenly couldn't see. Her glasses were steaming up.

The glasses were a brand new prescription that had come days after her thirty-fifth birthday—hardly the gift she'd expected. Still, it was nice to be able to read road signs, as well as the menu at her favorite taco stand. She'd actually been there a little more often, as of late.

Her pants probably weren't too happy about the change in her eyesight.

And neither would Lavina be when she saw her next. She'd been stressing ever since Elise had become engaged and kept pressuring her to make an appointment for a wedding dress fitting.

Not that Elise even cared about a dress. She'd already experienced the big wedding that ended with her ex committing adultery. No, she'd already been there, and done that. In fact, she'd be content to get married in the jeans she was wearing right now.

She skated past the opening to the space where the ice rink stored the Zamboni. The machine was tucked back in the shadows. Sitting up in the seat was a man. It looked like he was smiling, and she waved as she went by.

Elise wondered if he was getting ready to do some maintenance.

Her thoughts returned to her impending wedding. She may not want anything big and fancy, but if she didn't cool it with the tacos, she wouldn't even fit into her jeans. She'd be stuck wearing sweat pants for her wedding day.

I could always bedazzle them with the word 'bride.' Elise giggled to herself. She tugged off her glove and polished her glasses. Speaking of food, she was hungry. After two trips around, she was ready for a warm pretzel and glass of hot cocoa.

She scooted off the rink and found the snack shack. A bored attendant took her money. Elise thanked him and, wobbling on the skates, took her pretzel and cocoa to a table. She ate slowly as possible and then checked the time.

A groan escaped. She'd already been here over an hour. Brad was really late. He'd sent another text. —**Be there soon. It's no big deal. Someone's cat stuck in a tree.**

Don't they normally call the fire department for that? Elise grumped. *What's a police officer going to do, arrest it?*

She wobbled back out to the rink and started skating again. *Better get used to it. He's going to have this job for a long, long time. And I'm going to be his wife.*

She giggled at the thought. It still seemed so surreal to her. A lot sure could change in a year.

After a few more times around the rink, her ice skates smoothly slid across the ice, filling the air with a swooshing sound. She was getting it. It *was* like riding a bike.

She couldn't help it, memories of watching professional ice-skaters flashed through her mind. Did she dare? Her ankles felt secure in the boots, and she had some confidence after saving her balance a few times. She pushed away from the wall. With her hands out, she tried to make a graceful loop.

And, just like that, the wobbles intensified. She swung her arms for balance. Boom! She hit the ice rink hard.

There was no thought of being embarrassed, despite the group of tweens that glided by in laughter. Exploding pain stole the center stage of her concentration. One of the kids, a red-head girl in a pink pom-pom hat, yelled, "Be careful! This isn't for old people."

Her tail bone screamed too loudly for her to even respond.

"Honey, are you okay?" Out of nowhere, Brad swooped up next to her in a shower of slivered ice. *Oh sure, here I've been doing great for an hour, and the minute I fall, that's when he arrives.*

The dark-haired man squatted down next to her and balanced down on one knee. His hand reached to for her shoulder.

Elise's eyes squinted shut as she held her breath. She was afraid to release it for fear of the piercing scream that was clawing up her throat.

After a few moments, the pain began to lessen. "I can't believe you showed up in the nick of time to see me flop." She gave him a quick glance, her eyelashes wet with tears. Lovely. They left wet mascara marks on her glasses.

"I was hoping to surprise you, but you did it to me instead. That stunt was pretty amazing. I'd give it a ten," Brad said. He looped his hand under her arm and helped her up. She rose unsteadily. After she had her balance, he guided her over to the wall.

"I need a pillow," she whimpered. "Tied to my rear."

"I'll bet you do," he agreed. "That was some fall."

As soon as she reached the wall, she grabbed it and hung on tight. All she could think about was getting those cursed skates off. Her smeared eye glasses must really be broken because the rink's exit suddenly seemed miles away.

"I don't think I'm going to make it back," she mumbled.

"What's going on?" Brad's eyebrows raised in concern. "Did you hurt your ankle, or something?"

"No, just my tailbone." She frowned as he chuckled. "Go ahead and laugh. I thought I had enough padding back there but I guess not."

"Hmm," he said, taking a look at her bruised half. He gave a greedy smile.

Despite herself, she laughed. She pushed him away, teasingly, and then pulled herself along the wall. Now that initial shock of pain was gone, she noticed one of her ankles was throbbing, too.

"Great. Just great," she muttered, finally reaching the Zamboni opening again. She glanced inside, wondering if the guy was still in there. She'd probably given him a good show. He was probably laughing at her too.

Lovely. Yep. He was still there.

Elise gave the man a weak grin. The front of the machine reflected the overhead light back to her. The man had the same smile as before.

She looked closer.

The first vestiges of apprehension curled about in her chest.

She noticed his sunglasses seemed slightly askew. And why was he wearing sunglasses indoors anyway?

His head seemed at an odd angle.

"Brad?" Elise grabbed for her fiancé's arm.

"What?" He caught the look of alarm on her face. "What's hurting now? You okay?"

She shook her head, breathing rapidly. Brad slowly followed her gaze.

"Uh—" he began.

She interrupted him. "He hasn't moved since I last saw him. About thirty minutes ago."

They stared into the garage shadows. The man stared back. His grin was unwavering. And chilling.

"You all right with me leaving you?" Brad asked her. When she nodded, he skated for the Zamboni. Elise followed, hand over hand, pulling herself down the wall.

Brad paused when he reached the side of the machine. He called up to the man. "You okay, buddy?"

The man didn't move. As Elise got closer, she noticed his smile looked more like a grimace.

*He is decidedly **not** okay,* Elise thought.

Brad climbed up onto the foot rest and shook the man's arm.

It wasn't much of a shake, so it was a shock when the man slumped forward in the chair. Brad jerked in surprise, and then quickly felt for his pulse.

The scream that Elise had been holding in all this time erupted from behind her. Elise turned to look. It was the red-head girl in the pink pom-pom hat. The poor girl was shaking, her lips appearing like a red gash on her white face. Behind her gathered the rest of her friends, all wearing different expressions of shock.

Elise hesitated only a second before skating over to the girl.

"Are you okay? Here, sit down." Elise helped the swaying girl down to the ice. It wasn't ideal, but better than having her fall and split her head open. For a second, it was sketchy, and Elise wasn't sure if she was going to get the girl down gracefully, or tumble on top of her, but after a bit of flailing, they both were stable on the ice.

Brad came skating out of the Zamboni garage, cell phone to his ear. "Dispatch, we have a 187."

Elise's ears perked up at the code. After being with him this last year, she'd learned to recognize some of the lingo.

187. It was the code for homicide.

CHAPTER 2

The date was a disaster.

Of course it was. Some poor soul was dead, teens were skating about in different states of histrionics, and Brad was in full police mode.

Elise couldn't wait to leave the rink. After a crazy hour of the police interviews, yellow tape and the subsequent ambulance, the crowd of people rubbernecking at the removal of the body, and the noise and confusion, Elise was nearly jumping with joy to be freed to find her own car.

Her body felt drained from the adrenaline rush earlier. She started the Geo and jumped as the radio blared. She scrambled fast to turn it off. Finally, it was quiet.

Elise breathed in deep, eyes closed.

A tap on her glass both startled and annoyed her at the same time. It was Brad.

"You doing okay?" he asked, after she rolled the window down. His breath puffed in the cold air.

She nodded, and then gave the thumbs up when he didn't look convinced.

"Okay. I'll meet you there." He left for his cruiser. She turned the key and started her car. The engine lowered as it warmed up. She headed out, with him following.

After ice skating tonight, they'd planned to try the new Italian restaurant in town, but now neither one of them felt like eating. Elise knew she'd probably regret skipping the meal later, but her stomach was still churning from the sight of the dead body.

She pulled into her driveway and eyed the front door. Waiting inside was Lucy, a hyper sixteen-year-old. Elise knew the girl was just waiting to pounce on her the moment she walked in the door. That girl could really talk a person's ear off.

Elise adored Lucy but, at the moment, that was the last thing she wanted.

Brad pulled in and parked behind her. He must have

understood her hesitance because the next thing she knew, the passenger door had opened and he was dropping into the seat next to her.

"Are you sure you're doing okay?" he asked. Elise noticed his face looked worn and tired.

"I'm fine. What about you? You've had a long day," she said.

He leaned over to rest his head on her shoulder. Slowly, they wiggled until they were able to hug each other. She stroked his back and then up into his hair.

"You've been working a lot lately," she said. "I'm sorry we didn't get to have our date."

"I'm sorry I was late." His breath was warm on her neck. She felt his weariness in the way he relaxed into her. "And it's never good when a date ends with a dead body."

She shook her head. "No. No it isn't." Her fingers massaged his neck while she thought. "How did you know it was murder, anyway?"

He pulled back with a sigh. "People don't naturally die with pupils as large as his. And his neck was quite floppy. Did you notice that?"

Elise's stomached leaped at the word 'floppy'. She shook her head again.

"Yeah. And just a tiny bit of blood by his nose. Had his neck broken. There was a skate on the seat next to him. That's my guess."

"You're kidding?" Elise asked. "An ice-skate?"

He rubbed his jaw where his stubble was prominent. "Pretty unusual, I'll admit."

"And who would want to kill the ice maintenance guy? That seems so bizarre."

"Well, we can't just assume things, no matter how they appear. We need a positive ID on the victim. That's being worked on right now."

Elise frowned. "You don't think that's who he is?"

"He had on a Rolex watch. That seems a little rich for working at the ice rink. His shoes looked like they were designer. The heel wasn't worn, so they were new."

"How is that a clue?" Elise rested her cheek on the top of his head.

"It indicates someone who cares about his appearance and has the money to replace things often."

Elise's head slumped back onto the seat. She stared at the house again.

This time, someone was staring back. Her cat, Max, had climbed onto the window sill and watched her curiously. He'd been so scrawny when she'd first found him, but now he'd filled out to an enormous sixteen pounds of fluffy orange.

"Someone is waiting for you," Brad smirked, glancing up and seeing the cat. At that moment, the curtain pulled back even further, and a freckled face peered out. Lucy. The girl saw their car and waved, before disappearing back from sight.

"And she opens the door in three... two..." Brad counted.

The front door sprung open, and the tiny five-foot-two teenager stood in the doorway.

"Hi, guys!" Lucy yelled.

Elise chuckled. She turned to Brad. "The kids want our attention, I think."

"I guess so," he said. Slowly, they both got out of the car, like they were stiff and sore.

Truthfully, Elise was.

One of the "kids" in question was living with Elise temporarily. The teenager had been homeless and on the streets when Elise discovered her, having run away to escape a horrible home life.

But now things were changing. Lucy's mom had entered a treatment program and had been there for the last few months. The teen had yet to visit her, but the time was coming soon. Elise could feel it.

But for now, Elise had temporary custody. Poor Brad was dragged in by default. She glanced at her fiancé now, wondering how he really felt about that. He'd been very understanding at the time, but it couldn't be easy for him, going from being single for so long to a ready-made family.

And a teen to boot.

Elise hooked her fingers through his and they held hands as they walked toward the front door. She gave his hand a gentle squeeze. He returned it with a smile.

"What's going on in that mind of yours?" he asked, his eyebrow raising.

"Huh? What do you mean?"

"I can tell by your expression that your wheels are spinning. And not in a good way."

She laughed. "I was just curious if you're happy."

He stopped dead in his tracks and pulled her close. "Happy doesn't even begin to describe it, kid."

She rolled her eyes at his pet name "kid." He was exactly one month older than her. "You goof. You're the kid."

"I'm serious. I can't even believe you're mine. I'm still waiting for the moment you wake up and start screaming and run away." Again, his eyebrow rose. He leaned in close and gave her a kiss that had her nearly forgetting everything.

"You guys! Puke!" Lucy yelled from the doorway. The door slammed shut.

Brad was undeterred, but Elise pulled away laughing.

"Come on. Let's go in. I guess I'm hungry after all," she said. "I'm pretty sure I have frozen pizza."

"Mmm, frozen pizza. I've never had that before. I should give it a try," Brad teased. Just then, his phone rang. He glanced at the number and immediately switched into his professional voice.

"Carter, here." He repeated a few yes's, and mmhmm's while Elise watched curiously. Then said, "Thank you for letting me know."

He put his phone away. "That was the coroner. It looks like the cause of death is to be listed as broken neck. Most certainly brought on by blunt force, which the ice skate fits as the murder weapon. They're doing blood work, and that should be back soon. He was identified as Roger Hamilton. Sixty-three, lives at Ravondale Heights. His family owns the Hamilton Securities Bank where he works as the General Manager."

"Wow," Elise tried to digest the information. She reached for the door.

"Looks like we have a case, my dear Columbo," he said with a whistle.

CHAPTER 3

"*D*arlin', I don't know what to say. I feel like I can't even let you out of my sight for a moment without you discovering a dead body." Lavina frowned at Elise over her steaming cup of coffee. They were sitting in Kelli's Diner having a quick sandwich during Elise's lunch hour. It had been storming all day, making the light in the restaurant dark and gloomy.

"I'm sorry. Wait, what am I apologizing for?" Elise laughed and took a bite of her BLT. Her appetite was more than making up for disappearing yesterday.

Ignoring her, Lavina continued. "And *thee* Roger Hamilton. Loved by none, hated by all. The famous Ice-Man, loan shark himself. How do you do it?" She shook her head and rather daintily poked through her salad in search of a shrimp.

"As if I wanted to find a dead body!" Elise was starting to feel a bit indignant. "It wasn't exactly how I planned my date night, you know. Hair, check. Cute new hat, boots and gloves, check. Dead body, check."

"You have a skill," Lavina said sadly, shaking her head. "Of course, coroner's have skills too. Not ones most people want to excel in."

Elise rolled her eyes.

"Speaking of skills, I'm sorry to have to do this to you..." Lavina grabbed Elise's hand.

Elise instantly became nervous. What was Vi about to say? "What's the matter? Are you mad at me?"

"No, no. I'm not mad at you. But, as your best friend and maid of honor..." Her penciled eyebrow lifted at Elise's grin. "What's so funny about that?"

Elise hadn't actually asked her yet, but trust Lavina to take her rightful place.

"Something you want to say?" Lavina asked again.

Her fork was held up in a rather aggressive way. Elise chose a diplomatic reply. "It's just that I'm so glad you're going to be my maid of honor. I'm sorry I haven't formally asked yet."

Vi sighed. "Don't you remember the summer we were

fourteen? That sleep-over where we snuck the movie The Breakfast Club, which your mother said we were much too young to watch, and I brought over all the makeup I'd gotten from theater class. We did each other's make up and then promised each other that we would be each other's maid of honor. We sealed it with pinky promise." Brows raised at her excellent explanation, Lavina waited expectantly.

As Lavina had been talking, Elise did start to feel the flittering of that memory surface. "And Pogo..." she muttered.

"That's right. You had that darn beagle, Pogo. He ran off with my red lipstick. I think he ate it." Lavina scowled.

"He had red teeth for a week," Elise said with a shake of her head.

"I feel *so* sorry for him," Lavina quipped dryly. As if that reminded her, she removed a tiny jeweled compact from her purse and inspected her own lacquered lips.

Tucking it away, she continued, "Anyway, as I was saying, I'm sorry to do this, but we really need to firm up your wedding day. How can I possibly get everything together when I don't even know when it's going to be?" Her penciled-eyebrows drew together. "I just know you're going to spring the date on me and expect a miracle. Tell me you're not going to do that."

"No, nothing like that. I'll give you plenty of warning, I

promise." Elise held up her fingers like a girl scout. "We're honestly in no hurry."

Lavina looked at the hand sign, and the corner of her mouth quirked into a small smile. "I'm holding it to you then, lady."

Just then, a bright flash lit up the sky, followed by an explosion of thunder. The customers let out a collective squeal of surprise. Before they'd quieted, the power went out.

"Oh, crap," Elise said. Angel Lake wasn't known for speedy fixes of power outages. "I'd better head back to work." She pulled a twenty out of her wallet and slid it under her plate. "You know what the traffic is like when the power goes out. I guess I better stop at the store, too, for some TP and more candles."

ELISE INCHED her way down the road filled with cars, just as she'd feared, her windshield wipers beating back and forth in a losing battle against the heavy downpour. Where all the cars came from and why they magically seemed to appear the moment the traffic lights were out, she'd never know. None of them seemed to know how to navigate intersections without the green light telling them when to go. By the time she'd navigated through her fifth dead intersection, she was ready to scream.

They've come out with picture aps that can turn you into a deer. Why can't they come out with something for the lights when the power goes out?

The grocery store was crowded when she finally pulled into the lot. She found a space way in the back, and grumbled a bit, knowing she'd have to run in the rain.

But there was nothing for it. After pulling her purse strap over her shoulder, she grabbed her jacket and held it over her head. Then, with a deep breath, she darted out of the car.

The temperature had dropped. The rain was slushy and cold, and it seemed to laugh at her pitiful attempt to shield herself. Puddles splashed up as she ran through them.

Outside the store's entry were Christmas Trees wrapped in netting. The air smelled of fresh cut pine as she ran through the front doors. She nearly slipped on the slick linoleum inside. Yellow caution signs reminded her too late that the floor was wet.

The power was still not back on and the light of the store glowed a strange orange from the quarter-output of the emergency generator. She reached for a cart and threw her jacket into the basket, grimacing at the wet *twack* sound it made. Her hair hung in wet strings. She rubbed her sleeve over her forehead in an effort to dry it.

The aisles were filled with people scrambling to get last

minute items. The last time the town had a power outage, the shelves had been stripped nearly bare. Elise could feel her anxiety raising.

Just as she turned down the canned food aisle, a cart sharply connected with her ankle. Biting back a scream, she turned to see a grinning little kid.

"Tag! You're it!" he yelled.

The mother came running up, her face flushed. "Danny, we don't hit people. Say you're sorry."

Elise was so upset, she couldn't deal with an apology. She just gave a brief grin and walked away. *Limped away, is more like it.*

She loaded the cart with some soup and chili—easy things to heat over a camp stove—and went to pick up hot dogs. Along the way she added her needed toilet paper, a few cans of cat food, and some candles. She also grabbed a few boxes of pop tarts. For Lucy, she reasoned. Her tiny inner voice chose that moment to question who was she going to blame buying snacks on when Lucy returned to her mother's home, but she managed to squelch it.

As Elise browsed the hot dogs, she overheard a sharp male voice. She looked up to see a couple arguing. They were half hidden down the hallway to the bathrooms, and seemed oblivious to anyone around them.

It was the tall, pudgy, glasses guy from the ice-skate rentals. He was talking in a low voice to a woman, who was clearly upset.

She threw her hands in the air. "Well I won't have it! You know what happened!"

Wincing, he glanced around to see if anyone heard, his eyes locking with Elise's.

Elise turned back toward the hotdogs. She grabbed a couple packages, not caring about the brand any more, just trying to get out of there. Quickly, she pushed the cart down the aisle, but at the end, she couldn't help a glance back over her shoulder.

They were gone.

What a weird day. Shrugging, she got into line with Annie, an older blonde checker.

"Little Elise, how are you doing today?" The checker drawled. Her name tag on her shirt was framed in tiny plastic Christmas ornaments. In her hand was a paper and pen. Next to her was a calculator and an old-fashioned credit card machine.

"I'm tired and soaked. Traffic's crazy."

"So I've heard. Everyone coming in here is about as mad as wet hens. Kind of look like them too." The clerk pointed a skinny arm to the groceries. "Hon, just push your cart down here. Conveyer belt's not working."

Elise did as she was asked, and the clerk reached for Elise's items. Slowly, she wrote each item down on the paper and inputted it into the calculator.

"You hear about the Hamilton murder?" Annie asked.

Elise hadn't planned to engage in small-talk, wanting to get out of the store as fast as she could. But the fact that Annie knew it was murder intrigued her. The checker was always good for some gossip.

"I did hear about it. But how do you know for sure it was murder?"

"Of course it was," Annie smacked her gum. She looked at the toilet paper, and for one moment Elise thought she was going to tell her of a cheaper brand like she always did. Instead Annie must have felt pressure from the growing line because she just added the price without further comment. "Anyway, like I was saying, everyone knew his wife had it in for him."

"His wife?"

"Pure gold digger, that one. She was married once and had a son years ago. Husband died, and the son disappeared. So, ever since she came into his life two years ago, well, we've been waiting."

"You knew Mr. Hamilton?"

"Honey, I graduated with him. He was just as snooty back then as he was now. Couldn't stand to be outside his rich little neighborhood up in Ravondale Heights except to work at his bank. And he stepped on us, stepped on the very people who he'd grown up with."

"What do you mean, stepped on?"

"Well, rumor has it that he's in bed with a dirty trade company." She raised her eyebrows like Elise should get what that meant.

"Wow, that's horrible!" Elise said, faking.

"Yes, and part of the trade was some yo-yo mortgages. I know Grandma Babe's restaurant is about to go on the block because of one."

That bit of news made Elise gasp for real. Grandma Babe had brought her food like clockwork on every Wednesday from her restaurant for almost a year. The old woman always said she didn't want to see the skinny neighbor starve.

"She's going to lose it? Her restaurant?" Elise whispered, holding out her credit card.

"She certainly is, if Old Betty Lawrence is to be believed." Annie accepted the card and, with a grimace, tugged it through the manual credit card machine. "And she's never wrong."

Betty Lawrence went to The First St. Peters church and had been going for her entire life. She had her finger in every gossip pie and was known as Old Betty for as long as Elise knew her.

Elise wondered if there was something she could do to stop the restaurant from being foreclosed.

"Go ahead and sign, hun." Annie pushed the slip over to her.

Elise quickly signed it.

Annie read it before tearing off the back copy. "Such a pretty signature. You're lucky you're right-handed."

"I am?" Elise said with a laugh, taking the receipt.

"I just had someone in here who's signature was so bad it looked like chicken scratch. They told me it was because of being left handed. Anyway, here you go, hun. You have a good day, now."

After thanking Annie, Elise loaded her bags back into the cart. The rain pounded the pavement as she neared the exit doors. With a sigh, she lifted out the soggy coat from the cart and held it over her head.

Taking a couple deep breaths, she geared up to run. *Here we go!*

As she raced across the parking lot, a car started to pull out of its stall. It slammed its brakes, horn blaring at her. She glanced up to see a man scowling through the windshield at her.

It was the same grouchy man who'd been waiting at the ice-skate counter.

CHAPTER 4

*E*lise shivered as she pushed her rattling cart past the glaring man in the car. Slushy rain cut her visibility. Her breath fogged in the cold air. She glanced toward the passenger seat, but didn't see the woman he'd been arguing with in the store.

"Honestly, that guy needed to slow down," she grumbled as she reached her car. She flung open the trunk and tossed in the bags, hardly caring when one spilled. Now that the fear was gone, adrenaline was fueling her anger. She was starting to feel done. Done. Done.

The StraightenUp Chiropractic office was dark as she entered, but it didn't register as she shivered inside the doorway. *I'm completely soaked.*

Rubbing her arms, she hurried behind the desk and sat in her chair. Her damp clothes itched her skin. *Lovely. This is going to be a long, four more hours of being chilled to the bone.*

Elise turned the computer monitor on and frowned for a moment when it remained black.

Oh! Duh. The power is still off.

She smiled grimly. *Well, this is going to be interesting, seeing how screwed up billing is right now.*

Sue, her co-worker, came running through the front door, jacket half buttoned and her arms full. Sue was a short, thin woman. Her hair was cut just above her shoulders and had a sassy swing to it whenever she turned her head.

"Hey, lady." Elise smiled. "How was lunch?"

"Holy Toledo! It's practically a hurricane out there," Sue gasped. About ten years Elise's junior, this seemed to be her first official job after leaving the Peace Corps. She hurried to the back room where Elise heard the tumble of packages onto the back work table. Moments later, she came running back out, sans jacket, and smoothing her hair back in place.

The window panes shuddered. Elise looked to see the branches on the tree bowed in the wind. "It really is like a hurricane. Everything okay with you? We weren't able to talk this morning."

Sue fell into her chair with a huff. "I know, I was late." She tried to turn her monitor on and Elise giggled. Sue rolled her eyes. "Power's out. Duh."

"That's what I said," Elise admitted.

The girls laughed. "Anyway, it's been a horrible couple of days," Sue finished. She crossed her arms in front of her and tried to warm up.

"Oh, no! What happened?" Elise asked.

"My uncle died." Sue sighed. "The family's going crazy."

"What? I'm so sorry!" Elise said. Even as the words were tumbling out of her mouth, she suddenly had this sinking feeling.

"Yes, and you're not going to believe this," Sue continued. "He was murdered." She raised her brows, most likely expecting Elise to emit an expression of shock.

Elise *was* shocked, but not for the reason's Sue could expect.

"Did it happen at the ice rink?" Elise almost didn't want to hear Sue's answer.

Sue gasped. "Yes!"

Elise squeezed her eyes shut. The memory of that moment flashed in her mind. "I was the one who found him."

"What? Oh, Elise!"

The two women broke into, "I'm so sorry's," sounding in stereo. They both started to laugh, and then stopped, creating a bizarre moment for knowing how to react.

"I really am sorry," Sue finally said.

"Me, too," Elise agreed. "How are *you* doing? Do they have any ideas? Suspects?"

Sue reached into her purse for a tissue and blew her nose. "I'm doing okay. I really wasn't that close with him. I think they're suspicious of his wife. I know my mom is."

"Really?" Elise shook her head. "That's horrible! The poor woman."

"Speaking of my mom..." Sue got interrupted by the bell above the door jingled, alerting them to the first patient of the afternoon.

Both of them turned to the door, putting private talk away until the work day was over.

A FEW HOURS LATER, both Sue and Elise just wanted to go home. They were both freezing cold, and tired. Elise's eyes hurt from working in the dusky light all day.

Dr. Gregory, the chiropractor they worked for, sent them home soon after the last patient left, for which Elise was grateful.

Max was the first one to greet her in the dark, cold house. She frowned at the lack of the teenager yelling out a greeting from her room, like she usually did. *She must have gone home with a friend and forgotten to let me know.*

Elise set her groceries on the table with a thump. As she turned around, she let out a scream.

Standing in front of her was a moving bundle of quilts. Elise recognized Lucy's laugh from under the blankets. Even the teen's head was covered, leaving only a peep hole for her to peek out.

"Lucy! You goof."

"What? I got cold."

"Let me get some candles lit and then we'll see about starting a fire."

Elise's fireplace was more for vanity. The box only held one tiny log. But it would be better than nothing. She kept a box of fire-logs there just for this reason and soon had one lit. She rubbed her hands in front of the flames.

Lucy said, "You want to hear something weird? I was five before I realized dogs didn't purr."

"Well, that's random."

"I like being weird."

Elise laughed. She stood up and brushed off her hands. "Hey, you hungry?"

"Starving. Duh."

"All right, lets go figure out what there is to eat."

As the two walked into the kitchen, Elise broached a subject she knew Lucy had been avoiding. "Have you given any more thought to visiting your mom?"

A blush rose in Lucy's cheeks, blending in her freckles. "Sort of. The idea makes me nervous."

"I can understand that."

"Will you come if I decide to go?" Lucy looked up anxiously. Her dark eyes appeared huge on her face.

"I'll be there, if you want me to."

Lucy hugged Elise abruptly around the waist.

Momentarily surprised, Elise hugged the girl back. "Hey, it's going to be okay. Your mom seems like she's doing well. I mean, ninety days sober is a big deal. Longer, really..." She trailed off.

Lucy straightened and pushed tear-damp hair from her face. "You mean plus counting the time she was in jail, too?"

Elise hesitated and then nodded. "But I realized that didn't sound very nice."

"Nice?" Lucy sighed and went back to her bar stool. Elise watched her before grabbing out the box of cereal. "Nice doesn't describe anything she'd done before jail. Jail is probably the nicest part about it."

"I'm sorry, hun. Addiction is awful."

"Addiction is the devil," Lucy agreed, her eyes flaming with anger.

Ever since Lucy had been staying with her, Elise had taken her to weekly counseling appointments. The girl had gone through a lot. And honestly, even though her mom was in treatment, there was no guarantee that Lucy wouldn't be going through more. Elise wanted the teen to be able to get through it as best as possible. She really was a brilliant girl, and had her whole life ahead of her.

The rest of the evening was spent watching Lucy do her homework under flickering light, reading books under a blanket, and eating pop tarts.

Finally, Brad arrived. Elise sent Lucy off to bed, and cuddled with Brad on the couch. She shared with him about how the dead man had been Sue's uncle.

Brad groaned.

"What's the matter, she asked, resting her head on his chest.

"It's only a matter of time now," his voice was defeated.

"What do you mean?" she looked up at him.

"Until you're fully ensconced in this case."

"No! I'll never. Besides, I have other things on my mind." Elise said, settling back onto Brad's chest.

"And what's that?" amusement tinged his question.

"I guess we need to get to planning. Lavina won't leave me alone."

"Planning? You mean for the wedding?"

"Mmhmm," she answered.

"Well, I'm simple. I'd be happy to take you down to Las Vegas and elope. We could even have Elvis do it. But I know that's not what you want."

Elise rolled her eyes. "Dear heavens, not another Elvis." Elise had once taken a cruise with a bunch of Elvis's and wasn't keen on repeating that experience. She tucked her hair behind her ear. "I honestly don't know what I want."

"You have a yen for a big wedding?"

"No, no. Definitely not." Elise shuddered at the thought. "I'm actually thinking eloping doesn't sound so bad. But Lavina would kill me."

He laughed. "Actually, I think she'd kill me. She'd know that I put you up to it."

Max jumped up next to them. He climbed on Elise's lap, placing all of his weight on his two feet, and began kneading into her thigh. She moved him slightly.

"I really don't want to even think about it," she confessed. "It's so overwhelming." She glanced up and caught a flicker across his face as his eyebrows drew together. "Oh, shoot. That didn't come out right."

"Well, it didn't feel good to hear," he said. He let out a deep breath.

"I'm sorry. I didn't mean that to hurt you. It's not the marriage part. It's just having to invite everyone. The planning and figuring everything out."

"You're making this too complicated," he said, pulling her a little bit closer. He kissed the top of her head. "Let's just go down to the chapel and get hitched."

"Maybe we could do it on the beach at Angel Lake?" Elise

said. She could visualize herself there, the waves lapping at the shore. That was her favorite place in the whole world.

"Yes, exactly that. Just me, you and the pastor."

"And all the other people," Elise reminded him.

Brad stretched out his legs and flexed his feet. He rubbed his hand across his whiskered face. "Do we have to?"

Elise laughed. "My parents want to be there. You're the only son, so of course your parents want to come. Our friends..." She trailed off. That heavy, overwhelming weight was returning.

Maybe we should just jet off to Las Vegas?

"Listen, this is what we're going to do." Brad said, his voice firm. "We're going to get married in that little gazebo at the lake..."

"What if we can't get it reserved in time?" Elise was suddenly worried.

Brad wriggled around until he had his phone out. "I'm already on top of that," he said, and texted rapidly.

Elise felt a little bubble of excitement, watching him. "You have connections?"

"In city hall? You better believe it," he said as he pushed send.

"Besides, it's winter time. I'm not expecting we'll have a lot of competition."

Elise tried to relax as they waited for a response. She was getting more excited, and the feeling thrilled her.

Bzz! Brad's phone vibrated.

"It's her," he said as he read it.

"Oh, my gosh! That was fast. What did she say?"

"She says she's got us on the calendar. And she expects an invitation."

Elise covered her mouth, feeling both relieved and surreal. "It's happening," she whispered." She looked at her engagement ring, a rose setting, with tiny slivers of green emeralds for leaves. This was it. They were really doing this.

"Yes, it is. About time. You ready to become Mrs. Carter?"

She grinned at him. "Yes. How do you feel?"

"I feel like I've been waiting for this day my whole life." He rolled to his side, scooting her next to him, and wrapped his arm around her. "Let me tell you all the things I think about it," he said, whispering against her neck. "But I warn you," he kissed the skin. "It's going to take me a long, long time."

CHAPTER 5

*E*lise sat in Brad's running car with her phone plugged into his charger. She dialed up the heat and held her hand over the blowing vent.

I gotta do it.

She winced, bouncing the phone up in her hand. She could just picture Lavina's reaction when she heard the wedding news.

And she's going to kill me.

Sighing, she pulled up her friend's number and pushed send.

"You're calling. It must be an emergency," Lavina answered on fourth ring.

"Vi, Prepare yourself. Maybe you should sit down. It's happening. We have three weeks," Elise ripped off the bandaid and blurted out the news.

Her words were met with silence.

"Lavina?"

"Hold on, there, Ms. Pop-goes-the-weasel. I'm trying to process." Lavina's slow drawl held a bite of sarcasm. "I know you can't have just meant what you said, so there must be some sort of misunderstanding."

"Sorry. No misunderstanding." Silence. "What are you thinking?"

Her friend let out an exasperated sigh. "Girl, you promised me! How am I supposed to get the reception ready, get you a dress, and decorate in that time? What are you doing for invites? We need flowers.... You're asking for a miracle here."

"The key word is simple," Elise said. "I'm thinking of using the dress I got this summer. You know, the one—"

"No way on God's green earth are you going to wear that oops-a-daisy square dance dress. You will get a real wedding dress. We'll figure this out. After all, I happen to specialize in miracles." Lavina's pragmatic answer came back. "But, just so you know, you're mine for the next few weeks."

"I have to work!" Elise answered back with a laugh.

"You have lunches! You like protein bars? Because we're gonna be eating a lot of those!" was Lavina's response. "Now, where are you having it?"

"At the gazebo at Angel Lake. Brad reserved it last night. And, we're going to check Fabulous Flowers in town for any deals. Tamara is super nice. I'm sure she'll have something I can use."

"An outdoor wedding in the winter? You're set on that?" Lavina asked with just a hint of musing in her voice.

"Yes." The musing had Elise a little scared.

"I can just see it now. We could do capes. Fluffy, white fur lined capes. That would be so—"

"No." Elise said adamantly. "No fur-lined anything."

"*Faux* fur," Lavina emphasized. "Think of how cute that would be!"

"Right. We'd look like refugees from Little Red Ridinghood," Elise answered.

"Pish. Now tell me, who are your bridesmaids?"

"Well," Elise said slowly. She hadn't really thought about it. "I suppose just Lucy. Like I said, small and simple."

"Obviously, I'm your Maid of Honor."

"I know. I know."

"If only the power would come back on. I want to get you to Stella's place. Just wait until she gets her hands on you!"

"Stella?" The fear was real now.

"Yes, she runs the wedding boutique I was telling you about."

"All right, well I'm running back inside. I still have to get ready for work. I just wanted to let you know as soon as possible. My phone died, so I needed to charge it in Brad's car."

"Because your old car barely has enough power to run over a pop can, let alone charge a phone. You're going to need a bigger car when you two start having kids."

Elise's eyes popped wide open. "Lavina, don't even start. It's going to be a long, long time before I have kids." She shifted to look out the window at her car. "Speaking of kids, while you're petitioning for my time, keep in mind that I have to take Lucy out driving."

"Out driving, huh?"

"Yeah, she's in driver's ed at school. She's supposed to get sixty-five hours of drive time in."

"Good grief! Do they expect them to make a road trip or something?"

"Accumulative, Lavina. Don't you remember?"

"Darlin', I was practically born behind the wheel. I didn't take driver's ed. I just went to the DOL and made sure I scheduled with that blind old hermit, Mr. Jefferies."

"Vi! I don't want to hear that!"

"There's nothing to hear! Other than he could barely see and fell asleep about two minutes into the test. He passed me the first time through, though."

"Well, that was a long time ago."

Lavina huffed.

"A long, long, *long* time ago," Elise continued with a wicked grin.

"You be careful, missy. I'm planning your bachelorette party."

"Oh, no, no, no. Nothing like that."

"What? We have to party!"

"Nope, been there done that years ago. Simple, Vi, simple. I know it's a new concept for you, but there it is."

"Hmph. I might take that as a challenge. Anyway, I have to go, too. Have a lovely day at your job. I have a big order at the deli. I finally found someone with an appreciation of Serrano Ham."

"Okay, talk to you later. And remember, *simple!*"

Lavina had already hung up and missed that last word. Elise couldn't help but think her friend's timing was calculated just for that reason.

She stuck her hand in front of the heater for a second longer, wishing she could suck the heat in straight to her bones. She still couldn't shake her chill. After glancing at the time, she turned the car off.

Another wet, dreary day. And this time with no shower. She eyed her hair in the rearview mirror and made a face.

Back inside the house, still lit by flickering candlelight, she headed to her bathroom.

"I know I have dry shampoo around here somewhere..." she muttered.

"You looking for something?" Brad called from the kitchen. A moment later he was at the doorway, "Because I can hear you talking to yourself from out there."

By now, Elise had emptied the basket under her sink. She scrambled through the drawers. "Where is it? Did you use it?" She looked at him accusingly.

"No! Wait, what?" He threw his hands in the air.

"My dry shampoo."

He squinted at her. "You serious? I don't even know what that is, let alone use it."

"Um," a quiet voice came from behind Brad. He stepped back, bringing Lucy into view. "I think, I think I may have found it somehow, and used it."

Elise's eyebrow flickered. *Found it somehow?*

Lucy stepped forward with the pink aerosol can in hand. "Anyway, sorry about that. Here you go."

Elise took it and gave it a shake. *Almost empty. Perfect.* "You have plans for after school?" she asked, turning back to the mirror. She lifted her hair and sprayed the roots.

Lucy's face appeared behind her in the mirror. She shook her head.

Fluffing her hair out, Elise shook the can and sprayed some more. "Okay, we're having a driving lesson later. You game?"

Fear shone from Lucy's eyes. "Um...."

"You'll be fine. You're driving Betty. She's easy, and this will be fun. You'll see!"

"You scare me with your ideas of fun. Anyway, I'll see you later." Lucy grabbed her backpack and ran out the door for the school bus.

Just another day in paradise.

"How'd she take it?" Brad said showing back up at the door.

"Lavina or Lucy?" Elise asked. "They're both barely speaking to me at the moment."

Brad came with his cell phone in his hand. "Well, I have some news that will cheer you up. A little clue."

"A clue!" Elise immediately perked up. "And you're going to share it with me!" She spun around excited.

"I am. Only because I know you'll snoop it out sooner or later yourself. But you can tell no one."

"Of course!"

Brad laughed. "You should see your face. You look like you're about to get a present from Santa Claus."

"Tell me. Tell me. Tell me." Elise made grabby motions with her hands.

"Okay, here it is. The coroner found a note in his pocket. It was very specific. It said, 'meet me at The Cranshaw's at six o'clock. You will be very surprised.'"

"Really?" The Cranshaw's was a very expensive restaurant in Memphis. Not that Elise had ever been there. That's where the 'who's who' of the upper crust society went to be seen.

"And that's the time the coroner put his death."

"At six?"

Brad nodded. "So why was he at the ice rink instead of having a swanky meal?"

Elise pointed a finger in the air. "And who wrote the note?"

CHAPTER 6

After angling her car into the tiny employee parking stall outside the StraightenUp office, Elise eased the door open and poked out her umbrella. The rain had stopped during the night, but now had started up again with light patters on a saturated ground. The air smelled of the wet leaves that had been blown into scattered piles against the curb.

She locked the car and, huddled under the umbrella, hurried to the clinic.

The door was already unlocked when she tried it. Sue was waiting inside.

"Hi," Sue said brightly from behind the desk. It was a good

thing she said something, because she looked like a mound of laundry, swallowed up as she was inside a quilt. The office's counter was filled with flickering candles, making the room look cozy and scenting the air with vanilla.

"Hey," Elise shrugged off her jacket and hung it up on one of the hooks in the back office. She set the umbrella on the floor and then checked her hair in the mirror next to the door. Dry shampoo for the win! She walked back out into the office area. "How are you feeling, today?"

"Better," Sue said.

"Dr. Gregory already here?"

"Yep. He actually beat me in today."

"Hey, ladies!" came a deep voice from the back room. Stomping sounds next, and then the short chiropractor came through the push door. He grinned as he saw Elise. "How's the marathon training going?"

That's how Elise met Dr. Gregory. She'd wrenched her back a few weeks before the half-marathon that she'd trained for months for. He'd adjusted her spine and ribs, and after a few sessions, she was back to normal.

They'd discussed all sorts of aspects about training. He'd been running marathons for years so he had lots of good tips. And when the job had opened up, she'd applied without hesitation.

But now the marathon question made her groan. "I haven't been out running for a while," she admitted.

"You'll get back into it. When this weather's better," he nodded confidently.

"How are you going to convince your patients to lie down on a table when it's this cold in here?" Elise asked, shivering.

His grin got wider. "Now, don't get jealous, but I have a portable generator. It's running a space heater back there." As he mentioned it, Elise could hear the low rumble of the machine.

"I *am* jealous," Elise said, blowing into her hands. She hurried back to her jacket and retrieved a pair of gloves from the pocket. Her cute ones that she'd purchased specifically for the ice rink.

Dr. Gregory eyed them as she returned to the office. "Er. You guys can come back if you get too cold. Sue, when's our last appointment?"

Sue turned to scan the calendar, her hair flipping slightly. "Looks like three o'clock."

"Okay, so ladies, we just need to last until then. Think you can do it? We'll close shop after that." he said. "No need to suffer in case the phone rings."

The receptionists nodded.

Great! I can take Lucy driving even earlier. Elise walked to her seat. Waiting for her in the chair was a red-and-green striped fleece throw.

"I brought blankets," Sue said. "I thought you might like one."

"You are so awesome!" Elise immediately wrapped up in the blanket. She took a sniff, enjoying the floral fabric-softener scent. "Wow, I'm impressed! It's so clean, too. My blankets are always covered in cat hair."

"I'm feeling left out! Where's mine?" Dr. Gregory asked.

"Aw, I feel bad!" Sue said. "I didn't bring you one." The petite brunette made a sad face.

He chuckled. "I'm just kidding. Like I said, I've got the space heater. You guys enjoy your blankets. I actually needed to come out to cool down, anyway. It's so hot back there, I'm practically sweating."

Elise rolled her eyes.

The bell over the door rang and the day's first patient came in. Dr. Gregory greeted her. Then, first with a flicker, the lights flashed on, making everyone in the room cheer.

"Power's back!" Elise yelled. She laughed at herself. *Great job stating the obvious.*

"Mrs. Letterman," Dr. Gregory said to the patient, "You must be our good luck charm. Perfect timing. Come on back."

At noon, soon after the last patient for that morning left, Elise gathered her stuff up to go.

"You have lunch plans?" Sue asked.

"Yeah. Do you remember my friend, Lavina? She's helping me get ready for the wedding. I'm going to try to get together with her for lunch. What about you?"

"Wait, what's this? Did you guys finally set a date?"

"We did. Three weeks from now." Elise laughed at how Sue widened her eyes. "We're not crazy. I think it's half that we're easy going, and half that I'm ready to just get it over with."

"Oh yeah. Move on to the honeymoon," Sue said with a wink.

Elise paused. *The honeymoon? I completely forgot about that. What are we going to do? And there's Lucy....*

"Did I say something wrong?" Sue asked.

"What? Oh, no. You made me realize we'd never even discussed a honeymoon. I think I'm terrible at this getting married thing."

"It'll work out. These things always do. And what doesn't work out will turn into the best memory. At least that's what I've heard, from all those bridezilla TV shows. Who knows when I'll get married."

"You're so young. Take your time and remember it's okay to be choosy," Elise said. "I sure wish I'd been choosy my first time. I made a huge mistake and let someone in my heart that wasn't good for me. And it was hard to admit that."

"But now things are all better."

Elise laughed. "Not perfect, but yes, a million times better. And Brad's my best friend. I mean, what more can I ask?"

"It's nice to have someone have your back."

"He really does."

"Speaking of having someone's back," she hesitated. "I've been meaning to talk to you about something. I have a huge favor to ask of you, actually."

"Really?" Elise couldn't imagine what Sue could possibly ask for that would be so huge. "What?"

Sue picked at the front of her shirt. She cleared her throat.

"Just ask," Elise coaxed. "It can't be that bad."

"Oh, it is." Sue bit her lip. "So, uh, my sister is out of town. She's visiting her boyfriend."

"Okay?"

"Well, there's a family get-together tomorrow night. I never go to these without my sister." She nervously squeezed her hands together. "I know that sounds weird. It's not like my mom is mean or anything. But she's sharp. And when I'm around her all by myself, I'm the recipient of all the prickles."

"So, you want me there—"

"Just to be my back-up. You know, my wingman, so to speak." She gave a self-deprecating chuckle and tucked her hair behind an ear. "I know, that seems silly, but my mom gets me so upset my stomach gets in knots. I just can't do it alone."

"They won't mind me coming? Will they see my presence as an intrusion?"

"I don't think so. I hate to ask, but I'm desperate. It probably has to do with Uncle Hamilton's death so I can't just put her off."

Elise felt horrible at the anxiety in her friend's face. She couldn't relate. Her mom had always supported her, and was the best cheerleader she'd ever had, especially after the divorce. *What Sue must be going through to ask this....*

"Of course," Elise agreed. "I'd be happy to."

Sue grinned then, looking like a huge weight had lifted from her. That fueled Elise's suspicions even more.

What kind of family is this?

CHAPTER 7

*E*lise followed Sue out of the clinic. It was still sprinkling. Elise shivered under her jacket. "I'll see you later, okay?" she called as she ran for her car.

While she waited for it to warm up, she pulled out her phone. *Okay, first things first.* Elise quickly texted Lavina—**On my way to Grandma Babes. I'm starving. Want to meet me?**

Lavina texted back—**What about the protein bars?**

Elise snorted— **You eat them. I need real food.**

—**Fine, I'm on my way. You better be ready to make decisions. Or at least let me make them.**

Elise shook her head. The way that Lavina was carrying on, you'd think it was her getting married.

She put the car into drive, feeling her frown lines deepen.

Got to stop that. Those will be permanent. What is going on with Lavina though? She's always been bossy, but she's taking it to a whole new level.

Traffic in town was hardly better than yesterday, despite the fact that the traffic lights were now working. Elise could feel the tension building when she passed the construction signs. Always something. She found a spot right in front of the restaurant, under the cheery red-striped awning, and parked.

The power returning seemed to have called all the residents out for a hot meal, and the restaurant was packed. Elise glanced around for an empty table when an arm shaking in the air caught her attention.

She walked over to where Lavina was already sitting. "Hey. Where did you park? I didn't see your car?"

"Mr. G. dropped me off. I'll have you know I canceled lunch plans with him to meet you today."

"Aw, you didn't need to do that. I don't want to put you out. Like I said, I'm just aiming for simple."

A waitress wearing a blinking Christmas light necklace,

showed up then with two menus. Rather than look through them, Elise and Lavina ordered their favorites.

"And a glass of sweet tea!" Lavina added.

"Make that two. Is Grandma Babe working today?" Elise handed back her menu.

"She certainly is. Have you ever seen this place open without her?"

Elise smiled. "Would you ask her if she has a free minute could she please come to our table?"

"I'll definitely let her know." The waitress left, her shoes squeaking on the old linoleum floor.

Lavina hardly waited for the waitress to leave before she started in. "I have an appointment for a dress fitting with Stella at two this weekend. And flowers. What do you think of white roses? I think that would be divine for a winter wedding. As far as a menu, I was thinking roast turkey with all the fixings would fall into a winter season theme. I've contacted—"

"Wait! Hold up. What on earth is going on with you?"

"With me?" Lavina's eyebrows drew together in confusion. "What on earth is wrong with you? You're just sitting there, like a bump on a log, not taking any of this seriously."

"Look, all I'm saying is I don't want you to stress about the wedding."

"Well, apparently someone has to, or nothing will get done!" Lavina's cool tone held an edge that Elise wasn't used to hearing directed at her.

Just as she was about to respond, a cheery "Welcome, Ladies!" came from her left. Dressed in pink polyester pants with a large floral apron, Grandma Babe walked up to their table. "I heard you wanted to talk to me?"

The little old lady rested a wrinkled hand on Elise's shoulder. Her white hair seemed airy with its puffed curls. "You missing those Wednesday baskets?"

Elise recovered quickly and smiled up at the owner. "Best food I had in years. You had Brad spoiled and now I have to live up to it."

Laughter in the form of a soft wheeze came from the woman as her face scrunched into a hundred laugh wrinkles. "Oh, I'm sure you'll do just fine."

Elise couldn't help smiling back. "Thanks for coming out. I hope this isn't too personal, but I wanted to talk to you about something. I heard that the restaurant was being threatened? That it might close?"

Now Grandma Babe's face looked sad. Her eyes drooped like

a Precious Moments figurine. "Yes, that's true. My grandson's up here from Alabama trying to lend me a hand to salvage what I can."

"Is there nothing that can be done?" Elise asked.

"Not unless you can come up with a hundred grand. I have a balloon payment due at the end of the month."

Lavina gasped.

"It's that darn loan I got a few years ago. I took out an equity loan when the kitchen flooded and needed to be remodeled. Worst decision of my life. Mr. Hamilton had assured me that I could refinance at any time. But when I needed to do it, they said my credit wasn't good enough."

"How could your credit not be good enough? You own a restaurant."

Grandma Babe shook her head. "Between my age, a missed payment and being upside down on the loan, no one wants to lend to me."

"You took out a hundred thousand?" Lavina asked.

Grandma Babe snorted. "I took out fifty thousand. But somehow in the process, Mr. Hamilton turned my loan into an interest only. In fact, according to my nephew, I haven't even been paying the full interest every month. Fee's been doubling every few weeks. I owe a hundred grand now."

"Oh, my goodness. Didn't the banker disclose this?"

"That man didn't disclose a thing. Just gave me lots of smiles and told me how much he loved my pie. Oh, sure, my grandson is steaming mad. But what can we do about it now? Times change. I hear a fast food restaurant is already eyeing the place."

Elise felt sick at the thought of the iconic restaurant becoming a shill for cardboard-like burgers. "Can you get a lawyer to look at the contract? Maybe it's not legal?"

"We tried and lost. It's legal. He up and lied to my face. But it's all in the paperwork. Used to be a handshake was all it took to show honesty. Well he did take me with a handshake." Grandma Babe gave an angry sigh.

At that moment, Elise's phone vibrated. She took it out to read a message from Lucy. —**Elise, I'm sorry, but can you bring me a Tylenol? I have a horrible headache.**

She closed her eyes. One of the school rules was that the nurse could not give the kids Tylenol. It wasn't often, but when Lucy needed medicine, Elise had to drop everything and bring it out to her. And even that wasn't easy, between the calling the kid from class, filling out the sheet stating what medicine you were delivering, and finally handing it over.

Still, Lucy hardly ever asked, so Elise knew it had to be bad.

"Something wrong?" Grandma Babe asked.

"Yeah, I think I have to get my sandwich to go." Then, turning to Lavina, "I'm sorry. I have to cut this short. I've got to get down to the school."

Lavina looked down at the table when she said that. Elise could tell that Lavina was upset.

"We'll talk later, okay?" she asked her friend.

"Sure, we will, darlin'," Lavina answered, dryly.

"Your girlie okay?" Grandma Babe asked as she stepped back to let Elise out.

"She's not feeling well, but she's fine." Elise scooted out of the booth and walked over to the cash register. Grandma Babe caught the waitress as she was coming to deliver the food and sent her back to box up Elise's meal. Then she met Elise at the register.

"If you don't mind, I'm going to look into this to see if there's anything I can do," Elise said, as she passed over the twenty.

"You can try all you like, hun. You might want to team up with my grandson, Michael, as well. Like I said, he's piping mad."

Grandma Babe handed over the boxed food and the change.

"In fact, there's Michael right now. He just came in." She pointed with a gnarled finger.

Elise turned in that direction.

Standing by the door staring at her was the man from the ice rink. He was dressed nicer, in a three piece suit, but his face wore the same grouchy frown.

CHAPTER 8

"Michael!" Grandma Babe called. "Come over here,"

Instead of coming when Grandma Babe beckoned, the man pushed his way back outside.

"Well, that's odd," Grandma Babe said. "He must have forgotten something."

Elise accepted the change back and handed over a five for a tip. She wasn't so sure Michael forgot something. The expression in his eyes when he saw her was more of panic. That seemed like an action of avoidance at all costs.

As she returned to her car, she looked around, but didn't see him. She did see Lavina, however, watching her sadly out the window. She waved at her friend, and then made a funny face, hoping to cheer her up.

Vi shook her head as though shocked at Elise's infantile behavior. Well, that wasn't so odd, but the freak-out at the wedding planning sure was.

I really need to figure out what is going on with her.

At the school, Elise went through the song and dance to get Lucy her Tylenol. She sent Lavina a text asking when they could talk again, and then she was heading back to the office.

TRUE TO HIS WORD, Dr. Gregory let the two receptionists off at three. Sue was delighted, citing a huge laundry pile she needed to tackle.

Elise was ready for a long bath after a day like today. She checked her phone. So far, Vi hadn't answered.

Brad had texted though, asking that she call when she was on a break. She dialed him up.

"Hey, kid, I'm having a rough day," Brad said as he answered.

"Oh, no! What's wrong?"

"This investigation's hit its first road block," he grumbled. "The power outage—it might have worked in his favor."

"The murderer's? How's that?" Elise asked.

"Apparently, it short circuited the surveillance equipment at the rink. It was ancient equipment, it didn't stand a chance."

"But didn't that happen the next day...."

"Tell me about it," Brad growled. "Sometimes things move slow around here, and this is one of them. By the time the detectives went to check it out, it was too late."

"Oh, that really sucks."

"Yep. Chalk one point up to the murderer."

Elise could hear the discouragement in his voice. "It's going to be okay. You guys will figure it out."

"You bet we will. We always get the bad guy. Anyway, I'll talk to you later."

They said their goodbyes and hung up.

ELISE ARRIVED HOME JUST as Lucy was walking up the porch. The teen was mopey and tired. Elise left her petting Max to go jump in the shower.

Twenty minutes later, feeling scrubbed and in a comfortable t-shirt and leggings, she headed back to the living room.

Lucy still had not moved.

"Come on chickee. Let's get a snack."

With a moan, Lucy followed Elise into the kitchen.

"Tell me what you learned in school today." Elise poured her a glass of milk. She pushed over the cookie jar.

Lucy grabbed a chocolate chip cookie with her nose wrinkled. "That type of question ruins even a cookie."

Elise lifted an eyebrow. "Just give me the basics, Missy. How's your headache, by the way?"

"Head's fine, but it wasn't helped by the surprise test in marketing. By the way, Mr. Hamilton's name came up in class, today."

"Really?" Elise was surprised. "What did they say?" Max curled up against her leg with a little meow, not wanting to be forgotten.

"They were talking about business mottos, and how to make a good one. And how a good motto can outlive you. And my teacher asked if we'd heard about Mr. Hamilton. Like hardly any of the kids had. Then she asked if they knew the motto at the Hamilton Securities bank. It's a glacier on the door, with the words- Since nearly from the ice ages, we keep you solid. Almost half the class raised their hands."

That motto triggered something in Elise's memory. "Really! And how did they know that?"

The teen rolled her eyes. "Dude! It's right on the bank door every time you go in."

"Oh! That's right. Although, to be fair, it's not where I usually bank." Elise realized she read that motto when she dropped the StraightenUp money off and was impressed that Lucy remembered the motto.

Lucy shrugged and dipped her cookie in the milk.

"Now hurry up. We have a driving lesson to take before it gets dark."

Ignoring Lucy's groans, Elise scooped up Max and took him into the living room. On the way, she grabbed her phone from her purse.

Lavina weighed on her mind.

She settled into her window seat and waited for Max to decide if he was going to lie down. He did so, pinning one of her legs and making it impossible to get the other one in a comfortable position.

"Crazy cat," she whispered, scratching his ears.

He closed his eyes and broke into a deep purr. She couldn't help but smile at his contentment.

Maybe Lavina needs a pet?

She zipped a text off to her best friend. —**Sorry for running out on you again. I'll make it up to you.**

Lavina typed back—Tomorrow after work?

Tomorrow Elise was supposed to go with Sue to her family's house. **Elise sent—I have plans, but after dinner maybe!**

After that, she started an internet search on Grandma Babe's situation. Within a few minutes, she was discouraged. As unethical as the loan was, Elise couldn't find anything that could legally help.

"What's the matter?" Lucy said as she came in the living room. She was French-braiding her hair as she walked, a trick Elise could barely master in front of the mirror.

"Oh, I just need to figure out how to get a hundred thousand dollars in a few weeks. No big deal."

"Did you try setting up a Go-Fund-Me?" the teen asked, twisting a bit to examine the braid's tip. She fished a rubber band from her pocket and tied off the end.

A Go-Fund-Me! Of course! "Do you think I could get enough people's attention to it?"

"What's it for?" Lucy asked.

Quickly, Elise explained Grandma Babe's situation.

"Our student government would totally support that! We can print flyers, even."

"Seriously!" Elise was excited. Lucy came over and together they set up the charity fund.

"That's it then, I'm done for the day," Lucy said, when Elise closed the browser.

"Not so fast. Go get your permit. It's time to drive the wild thing."

Lucy groaned. "Fine. Just take me someplace where no one I know will see me."

Elise mock-glared at the girl. "You be nice to my car. She's a classic."

"You don't have to tell me," Lucy muttered on her way to her room. "A classic piece of..."

"Lucy!"

"Beauty! I was going to say beauty!" Lucy yelled, before slamming her door.

TEN MINUTES LATER, they were firmly seat belted into the

front seats of the Geo. And by 'firmly' Elise meant her knuckles were white as she gripped the handle above the door.

Lucy had narrowly missed hitting the mailbox as she'd pulled onto the street. She'd swerved hard, nearly side-swiping a parked car. She'd slammed on her brakes and stared at Elise.

"What do I do, now?" she whispered.

"So that was called over correcting." Elise said. "Now we're just going to back up, nice and gentle." She turned in her seat to peer out the back window.

"Nice and gentle," Lucy echoed.

Elise felt the car shift as Lucy put it into reverse. She watched carefully out the rear window while the teen stepped on the gas.

"Wrong way!" Elise yelled, as the car lurched forward. Lucy slammed on the brakes.

The seatbelt jerked to lock again, making Elise grimace.

"Sorry! I'm no good at this!" Lucy wailed.

For a second, Elise wanted to agree. After all, they were just trying to get down a straight road. But the road was narrow, with cars parked on both sides.

Elise eased a finger under the seatbelt trying to loosen it.

"Don't worry. One day we're going to look back at this and laugh." She tried to bolster her shaky tone with a little laugh.

"One... day," Lucy agreed. She chewed on her bottom lip.

Elise tried again. "Keep your eyes up ahead a little bit. Don't be looking right at the end of your hood. You've got this."

Finally, Lucy had the car in the right direction. They drove silently for a few minutes, and then Elise had her turn down a country road with low traffic. After ten minutes, Elise could see the teen relaxing.

"Lucy, you're doing great. You feeling up to me asking you a question?"

The girl nodded.

"What do you think about meeting your mom? You've been having good conversations on the phone. You know, she's been asking."

Lucy bit her the inside of her cheek. Elise waited, letting the girl think.

It was when she started to sniffle that Elise knew something was wrong.

"Okay, pull over there." Elise hurriedly directed to the side of the road. The car bumped in the grass. "What's the matter, hun?"

The girl shook her head, her lips pressed together. Tears started to fall.

"What's going on?"

"Is it because you want to get rid of me?"

The words were like a knife in Elise's heart. "No, no, nothing like that. You're welcome to live with us until you go to college. And you will go to college, because life has big plans for you!"

"I thought... because you and Brad..."

"No, you are my family. But your mom is your family, too. And the counselor thinks she is a safe person for you now. There might be things you guys can work on, so you both get some healing. But you don't have to. Only when you feel the time is right. Which is why I'm asking."

"Will you go with me?" Lucy's voice was tiny and vulnerable.

"Of course. But you are going to kick butt and take names. You're going to be okay."

Lucy smiled at that. "All right, I'll let Mom's counselor set up a time. But, I'm warning you. I still might be a nervous wreck."

"That's okay. You can feel anxious, just don't camp out there. Now you ready to get back on the road, again?"

Lucy nodded. She put the car back in drive and then gave it too much gas, and the back tires of the Geo squealed.

"Wow! I had no idea this baby could do that!" Elise exclaimed. "Careful there, Mario Andretti."

"Sorry!" Lucy yelled. She looked a bit more relaxed behind the wheel though, and they sped away, making the leaves flutter behind them.

CHAPTER 9

*E*lise puzzled all the next day over Michael. Why had Grandma Babe's grandson been at the ice rink? She'd shared her run-in with Brad, and he'd passed it on to the lead investigator. For a moment there was a flurry of excitement. It seemed like it was a solid lead.

Until Brad shared that Michael had been happy to cooperate with the police. Apparently, it was a coincidence he was there the afternoon of the murder. Being new in town and searching for a job, it was one of the places where he'd stopped to pick up a job application.

Brad said they weren't ruling him out, but were starting to focus on the new wife. And there was a new suspect they'd just uncovered, one that he wasn't at liberty to discuss, yet.

"You're going with Sue tonight, right? Let me know what you make of the Hamilton family," he'd said. "Detective Miller is very interested in your opinions."

"Really! He wants my opinion?"

He winked. "Like we really were going to get a choice. I told him we had a Columbo on our hands with you."

At the clinic, Sue seemed at an unusually high energy all day. After work, she followed Elise home, where Elise dropped off her car and then hopped into Sue's. Her car was a newer rattle trap version of Elise's two-door white Geo. Elise snorted at the "sport edition" emblazoned on the back.

"Here we go around the mulberry bush!" Sue's singing voice was high and almost manic.

Elise glanced sharply at her.

"Sorry, sorry. I think seeing my mom makes me a little crazy." Sue flushed, looking more than a little abashed.

"It's going to be okay. I'll be there."

"If she says anything...odd. Just go with it. She can be so snippy that it's best not to engage," Sue warned.

Well, this sounds like the epitome of fun.

It was cold tonight, and Elise was surprised to see the

headlights picking up snowflakes. Wet splats hit the windshield.

"It's snowing!" Elise exclaimed.

"I hope it doesn't stick." Sue turned on her wipers.

Elise didn't think it would. She loved driving at night watching the snow fall.

The road took them out of Angel Lake and up into Fairview. This city was known for its wealthy residents. Elise remembered hearing that Mr. Hamilton lived in Ravondale Heights and wondered if she'd finally get a chance to see the exclusive neighborhood.

Excitement prickled as Sue turned down the fabled street. A guard sat at the entrance, nodding when Sue showed him her ID. The gate slowly opened, and Elise felt like she was about to enter OZ.

She was not disappointed. These people had money, but nothing could have prepared her for the ostentatious Christmas displays. Replications of old globe street lamps lined the street, festooned with clear fairy lights. What must have equaled miles of lights, drew sparkling lines around every curve of the mansions, from the eaves to the columns. Elise couldn't even imagine their power bill.

Still, there was nothing garish about the displays. No flashing lights, no inflatables in the front yard, or fake candy canes. Just twinkling lights that almost seemed artistic in the way they highlighted the houses' towers, portcullis, and grand entrances.

"It's magical," Elise breathed.

"It's one of my favorite things to see," Sue agreed.

They pulled down a driveway of a house even larger than the rest.

"Your uncle's?" Elise asked.

"He lives...used to live up the road. This was my grandfather's home before he passed. Now it's my mom and aunt's."

Elise scanned the front of the mansion. What an opposite lifestyle Sue must have led before she entered the Peace Corps. She wanted to hear more of that story, one day. "Your uncle didn't get a share of the property?"

"Both he and his brother got a portion of the partnership at the bank. He already had enough money to buy a house just up the street."

She parked the car next to a Lincoln and a Rolls Royce.

"You ready?" Elise asked. She was more than ready to clap eyes on just what roots Mr. Hamilton came from.

Sue nodded, and they exited the car. This house wasn't covered in white lights, like so many others. Instead huge vases, the size of a small car, held an overflowing amount of white flowers. Tiny red flowers were interspersed among them. The scent was heavenly as they walked up the steps.

At the front door, Sue seemed to hang back, bringing Elise to an awkward stop behind her. She waited to see what her friend would do.

Finally, Sue squared her shoulders and took a deep breath. Without another delay, she wrenched opened the door and walked in.

Elise's imagination had been on overdrive for this moment, picturing how it would go. She knew the family terrified Sue, so images of a real life Cruella, or perhaps Meryl Streep from *Devil Wears Prada* doppelgänger were what she was expecting.

But she wasn't prepared for the quiet of the room. Although every seat was filled, the people sat as though they were a part of a museum exhibit. Five heads—three men and two women —swiveled as the two women entered, every eye trained in their direction.

No one greeted them

Elise suppressed a shiver as she shut the door. No wonder Sue had been nervous.

A clicking broke the quiet as a miniature poodle trotted toward them. Its nails clacked against the wood floor. The noise was such a relief that it made Elise suddenly conscious of the fact that she was still hanging on to the door knob. She released it and clasped her hands behind her back.

"Hello, Mother," Sue said.

Elise felt her eyebrows flicker at the distinct change in Sue's voice. It had always been soft, but now there was a pleading quality in it that Elise had never heard before. Her heart felt torn and her gaze dropped to the floor.

"Susan," one of the women answered, her voice tightly caught between distaste and obligation. She wore a pale blue silk blouse and linen pants. "How lovely that you brought a friend." Her tone indicated it was anything but lovely.

The dog began to sniff at Elise's shoes. The animal's pure-white fur had been groomed into puffs, with two pink bows at the ears. Its black nose flared as the dog caught an interesting scent, possibly of her cat, Max.

Elise squatted down and offered her hand for inspection. The dog gave it a polite sniff and then stared up into Elise's eyes. He panted a doggy smile and Elise reached out to stroke the pup's cheek.

"Cookie! Come here, girl." Sue's mother's sharp command

made Elise jerk. The dog reacted the same way and cowered by Elise's feet. "Cookie!" the woman snapped her fingers.

The dog scurried back to its owner, the nails making more of a scrabbly sound rather than the confident clicks it had when first crossing the room. Cookie then disappeared under the ornate coffee table presumably to huddle by her owner's feet.

Sue stood in the same spot she'd taken when she'd entered. Arms stiffly at her sides, her shoulders back. But Elise could see the edge of her skirt was trembling. This girl was struggling. Elise got to her feet and took a few steps closer, hoping her physical presence would help her friend.

"Well, now. Aren't you going to at least introduce us? To your friend?" The mother's voice took a fake playful quality. "I taught you better manners than that."

Sue jerked as if hit by a live wire. "Of course. Mother, this is Elise Pepper. Elise, this is my mom, Ms. Christoff."

The woman nodded, her brunette hair a stiff helmet of carefully placed waves.

"And this," Sue waved her hand, "is my Aunt Delores, Mrs. Terrington."

Dark haired like her sister, the tiny woman perched on the end of the couch as if the furniture's back was fitted with spikes. Her ankles were neatly crossed. She gave Elise a nod with a slightly raised eyebrow.

There were more people to introduce, but before Sue could get to them, her mother interrupted. "Well." Ms. Christoff's sharp gaze moved from Elise to Sue. She stared at her daughter while Sue shifted uncomfortably. "This day certainly has had its fill of uninvited guests. I suppose I should make some introductions myself." She stared at a man seated at the other end of the room.

CHAPTER 10

The man was in his late forties, his dark hair styled conservatively. At Ms. Christoff's glanced, he stood up. Elise immediately noticed he was very tall and wore a fitted, gray three-piece suit. He motioned to a young twenty-something man sitting next to him. As he did, his sleeve pulled up just a bit to give a peek of a tattoo. "Come on."

The young man stood up. He wore a sports jacket and dark blue jeans. His hair was longish and almost black. It curled slightly where the tips met his collar. He was also tall, although not as tall as the man standing next to him.

Ms. Christoff glanced cooly at him. "Susan, this is your cousin, Parker."

"My...cousin?" Sue's hair swung gently as she turned to study the young man.

"Hello, Susan. It's so nice to meet you," he said, his voice shaded with a deep English accent.

"Err, hello." Sue turned all shades of red as she looked back toward her mom. She said softly, "I didn't realize I had a cousin, Parker."

"He's been estranged from the family," Ms. Christoff reached for one of the consolation cards on the coffee table and fanned herself. She seemed a little uncertain as she finished her explanation. "He's your uncle Roger's son."

Sue's mouth dropped open. Her mother arched an eyebrow and cleared her throat.

"Let me explain," the well-dressed man said. He glanced at Elise. "Henry Bingham, of Bingham Attorneys of law."

"He's our family's counsel. His family has always handled our business," Ms. Christoff added.

"Approximately one year ago, I was contacted by a Barrister Edwards from East Sussex, and given a letter. He represented the estate of Katherine Stuart, this young man's late mother. The letter held a copy of a photograph of a much younger, Roger Hamilton and an equally youthful woman. The letter introduced Master Parker, formally presenting him as Mr. Hamilton's son."

Sue's head swiveled between the attorney and her mother.

"Susan, must you stand there with your mouth open that way?" her mother asked.

"I—I'm sorry," Sue said. "I'm just a little overwhelmed."

"It's understandable." Parker dipped his head in acknowledgement. "I only found out shortly ago, myself."

"While Mr. Hamilton regrettably did not meet his son, arrangements were made for a DNA test to be taken. The results of the test were 99.987 percent. Unfortunately, Mr. Hamilton passed before he could make his son's acquaintance, but he did want to do right by him."

Mr. Bingham tilted his chin. "It's because of that duty that I had the sad responsibility of notifying Parker that his father had passed before he had a chance to meet him. I arranged for him to fly out, and met Parker's plane yesterday. We've been staying at the Presardio in Angel Lake. With the power outage, it wasn't quite the welcome I'd hoped America would give him. I wanted him here when I called this meeting. It's time for me to read the amendment that's been made to the will."

At this news, several members of the family gasped.

One man yelled, "This is an outrage!"

Mr. Bingham eyed him calmly. "Since I haven't read it, there's no need to be outraged just yet. We are waiting for one more concerned party."

Sue looked around the room. "Where is Claudia?"

"She's late." Ms. Christoff stated. "Surprise. Surprise."

Elise wondered what was going to happen next. *Who's Claudia, and are we just going to stand here and wait?*

"So, how did you meet your friend?" Ms. Christoff asked, this time staring pointedly at Elise.

Sue flushed. "I work with her. At the clinic."

"Oh," Ms. Christoff's scrutiny sharpened. Elise shifted and offered a smile.

Ms. Christoff did not smile back.

"Well, now, that's nice. Isn't that nice?" Mrs. Terrington, her sister said, nudging her sister.

A cold smile flickered across Ms. Christoff's face, disappearing as fast as a dusting of snow in sunlight. "Very."

Elise swallowed hard. Darn it if she didn't feel like the mongoose in the viper's nest.

Everyone's attention was grabbed by the sound of the front door opening. Elise joined them in facing the doorway.

"Hello! Hello! Anyone miss me?" A high tinkling laugh came first, ushering in a woman in her forties. Her hair was a halo of blonde frizzy curls, held back by a ribbon. She wore a red fitted dress that emphasized her large bust.

"Claudia," Ms. Christoff snipped, "You're late."

"Oh, well nothing's going to happen without the widow!" Claudia Hamilton introduced herself with a laugh.

Elise was surprised at her candor. Claudia grinned cheekily like she knew everyone was shocked.

"Mr. Bingham! So nice to see you. He was the one who introduced Mr. Hamilton and myself." The more she spoke, the more obvious it was that her voice was slightly slurred.

"Mrs. Hamilton." The lawyer bowed his head toward her.

"I'm glad you could find time to welcome your husband's son." Ms. Christoff slid back into the couch with a satisfied smile. It seemed this was a nugget she'd been waiting to deliver.

"Parker? He's here?" Claudia scanned the faces.

Elise was surprised when the widow's glance skipped past Parker.

"You've already been acquainted with him?" Ms. Christoff asked, her smile slipping. Her eyes narrowed.

"Of course! Poor Roger has been in contact with Parker ever since he found out he was his father."

Parker walked forward just then. It seemed to Elise that he was hesitant. When he saw that Claudia caught sight of him, his chin lowered.

"Claudia," he said. "After all those phone calls...it's so nice to finally meet you face to face."

Mr. Hamilton's widow stared. Her head shook slightly side to side as if in disbelief. Then, she slowly held out a hand.

He took her hand in his and shook it.

"Parker," she said quietly. "I'm so sorry for your loss."

"We have a lot of catching up to do, it seems. There will be plenty of time. I'll make sure of it," the young man answered.

Elise could feel her eyes widen. Was it just her imagination? Or did those statements carry with them a threat?

CHAPTER 11

"Are we ready for me to read the amendment?" the attorney, Mr. Bingham asked. He waited for everyone's attention and then pulled a pair of reading glasses from his front pocket. "As you all may remember, the old will stated that should he pass with no living children, his wife would receive thirty percent of his estate, and his living siblings the remainder.

A leather dossier sat on the table before him, which he opened. After shuffling through a few sheets of paper, he read out loud.

"'As I reach an age where fatherhood seems out of the cards for me, simply because I do not have the desire to parent small children, I find luck has bestowed an unexpected gift on me. A son.

"'I met Miss Katherine Stuart nearly twenty-five years ago. She was to be my constant companion during the months I spent in England. We parted ways when I returned home, and I have not been in contact since.'" At this point the lawyer shuffled through the papers before finding a photograph and holding it up for the family to see.

He continued. "'In November of this year, my attorney, Henry Bingham informed me of a letter he'd received from a Barrister representing Katherine Stuart's estate. Sadly, she'd passed the month before from an unexpected illness, but not before leaving a letter addressed to me.

"'In this letter, I learned I had a son of twenty-four years of age. He was introduced to me as Parker Roger Stuart.

"'My attorney procured the proper tests to establish paternity rights. And as that came back as conclusive, I've endeavored to make contact with the boy.

"'I'm making the statement that I, Roger Carter Hamilton, amend this will to the following.

"'My dear Claudia to receive thirty percent, my living child(ren) to split forty percent, and my company to receive the remainder held as a trust for my child(ren). Any living siblings will split ten percent of the stock holdings in Hamilton Banking.

"'If any should contest this will, they will receive nothing.

Signed, Roger Carter Hamilton. Notarized by Mrs. Johnson,'"

Mr. Bingham removed his glasses and tucked them away. He refolded the papers, giving the tattoo a chance to peek out from the cuff again. Elise had a longer look at it this time. The edges were blurred as if it were old.

"Mrs. Johnson," Ms. Christoff mused, her lip curling into a cold grin. "Funny how she didn't mention that to me in all this time." She glanced at her sister. "We have the same manicurist."

"I do have some good news," Mr. Bingham said. He raised his voice when the group ignored him. "I said, I have good news."

Finally, everyone quieted.

"We've been successfully able to block a petition at the Office of Inspector General of the FDIC for an audit with the claims of predatory lending. The Inspector General overthrew the petition on grounds it was biased."

"Who brought the petition?" Elise asked. Again, twelve pairs of eyes fastened on her. The stares made her sweat, but she straightened her spine and tried to force a confident look in her eye.

"Ms. Christoff?" Mr. Bingham deferred to his client.

"I really don't see the need...."

"It was a Mr. Michael Baker, right? Aunt Babe's grandson," Sue's voice rang out loud and clear. Her chin stuck out defiantly.

Mr. Bingham glanced again in Ms. Christoff's direction. His tongue dabbed against his bottom lip. "That is correct, Miss Christoff."

Sue glanced at Elise and smiled.

"I don't know what you're smiling about, Susan," Ms. Christoff buffed her nails and then examined them. "Maybe you don't understand what all of this means."

"Would you care to explain, Mother?" Sue's voice had dipped back into the meek. Her shoulders rounded under the angora sweater she wore.

"Don't be a ninny. The law suit being dropped means next to nothing. The amendment to the will means your inheritance is nearly gone."

"You mean yours, Uncle Jeff's, and Aunt Delores..."

"We were to get twenty percent each. Naturally, some of that would trickle down to you. Though, now this 'amendment' puts a wrench in it all. I suppose the will be stuck in probate forever."

"Are you sure you want to do that, Ms. Christoff? The will is quite clear that whoever tries to contest it, shall inherit nothing."

"Of course we will," her mother snapped.

"Ten percent of a mega million dollar estate is better than nothing," the lawyer hedged. He put his hands in his pocket and stared down his nose at her.

"And how do we know he's really his son?" Ms. Christoff's thin arm waved in the direction of the young man. Deep wrinkles appeared around Ms. Christoff's mouth as if she'd bitten into a lemon.

"I assure you, he's been checked and double checked. You may examine a copy of the DNA analysis." The lawyer's voice was low as he answered.

No one looked at the young man in question, except for Elise. His skin was flushed, and he stared down at his shiny, most likely new, wingtips.

"Well, Claudia can't like that much either," Sue mused. She walked to the sideboard and reached for the decanter.

"Will you put that down? That's what we have housekeeping for."

Sue jerked as if she'd been jolted by a cow prod. Shakily, she set the bottle down. It clattered slightly on the counter.

"And as for Claudia," the mother continued. "What does she care? He could have fifty sons for all she cares. She still gets her cut no matter what."

"I'm standing right here," Claudia said with a drawl. She walked over to Sue. "And I'll think I'll have what you're having." She placed two shot glasses on the counter and uncorked the brandy.

Elise winced at the word, "cut," making it sound like it was a stock holders' meeting discussing a company being sold.

"Something seems shady about all of this," said Mrs. Terrington. "Who's the executer? Where's the notary public?? I'd like to question her."

"Mrs. Johnson. You'll find her at the bank," Ms. Christoff said, picking up the condolence card and waving it again. "I'd like to chat with her, myself. I'm sure there's no conflict of interest, seeing as how she's the manager of Hamilton Bank. And just who exactly is the executer." Her head jerked in the lawyer's direction, shooting him a look that could kill.

Mr. Bingham blanched but held his ground. "Everything was signed in the most aboveboard manner. And, as was always the case, I remain the executer of both the old will, as well as the amended version."

"Very interesting. All signed aboveboard, snug as a bug, you say? More than I can say about some of the loans you oversaw," Ms. Christoff stared him down. "Maybe we should be talking more about that."

"I don't see what past loans has to do with anything. And if you'd like to discuss that, please come to my office." Mr. Bingham pulled out a pocket watch. After examining it, he clicked it shut. "And with that, I need to be going. Good night to you." He nodded his head and briskly walked out the door, leaving the dossier on the table.

Poor Parker watched him go like a piglet being left by its mother. He turned to the rest of the family, who studied him like a pack of hungry wolves.

CHAPTER 12

Sweat sprouted on Parker's brow as everyone watched him. "Listen, I can only imagine your shock. I think I should be going as well."

"Nonsense," said Ms. Christoff, her tone infused with fake delight. "We need to get to know you better. After all, you're family. And dinner will be ready soon."

"I agree," the widowed Mrs. Hamilton said. She walked up to him and curled her fingers around his upper arm. "My! They fed you well in...where was it again?"

"East Sussex." His voice cracked like his mouth was dry. Gone was the warning tone Elise had thought she'd heard earlier. Now the roles definitely seemed reversed.

"Mother, I wasn't planning on staying for dinner. I need to get Elise home as well. She has dinner plans." Sue said.

"What is all this talk about going?" Mrs. Terrington exclaimed. "My goodness, Sister, did you ever?"

"Everyone is staying, and that's final." Ms. Christoff's cold gray eyes swept around the room, finally landing on Elise. "Except for her, of course. If she needs to leave, then we'll call her a cab."

Sue opened her mouth like a fish. Her face went white with panic. It was obvious she didn't know what to say. "Can you change your dinner plans?" she asked, her hand reaching for Elise's arm.

Elise didn't need to feel the strength of the grip to realize Sue was begging. "Sure, just give me a second," she said. She dug out her phone from her purse.

Oh, boy. Lavina's not going to be happy. But I can't leave this poor girl here, alone. She sent the text to Lavina postponing the wedding-planning get together.

It wasn't ten seconds later that Lavina responded, all in angry caps—**YOU BETTER HAVE A GOOD REASON GIRL!**

Elise responded— **I do**

Lavina said— **Good, because the next time you cancel, you're going to end up with a canary yellow dress and fur-collared capes!**

Elise smiled as she tucked her phone away. She looked up to see everyone watching her. "Uh, it's fine. I've rescheduled my plans."

"Wonderful." Ms. Christoff's tone said it was anything but.

Elise crouched on the ground and made a soft kissy noise to the dog. "Cookie. Come here, girl."

The dog scooted over from where she'd been sitting at the base of the couch. Her tail wagged slowly as if uncertain. Elise held out her fingers for the dog to smell and, when that seemed to go well, began rubbing the dog behind her ear. "What a pretty girl you are," she whispered.

"I'd like to see the picture. Where's it at?" Mrs. Terrington said. The leather dossier was located, and the contents examined.

"Copies, nothing but copies," Ms. Christoff said dismissively.

"Well, you sure can't imagine he'd bring the real documents here to these heathens," Mrs. Terrington added.

Elise was delighted and surprised when the picture made its rounds to her.

Sue whispered, "I'm so sorry about all of this," when she passed it over.

"Oh, don't worry. I'm totally fine." Elise said. She examined the picture. Like Sue's aunt had mentioned, it was a copy of the original. Across the bottom, in backward slant, were the words, *Roger and Catherine, East Sussex.*

"Did you hear he was supposed to meet with someone? That day he went to the ice rink," Elise whispered to Sue. She hoped by feeding Sue that little bit of information, her friend might be able to ferret out who her Uncle was supposed to get together with.

"No?" Her friend shook her head, looking worried.

"Yeah, at the Cranshaw's." Elise leaned in closer. "I'm not sure I'm supposed to know. Maybe you can ask around?"

Sue nodded. She plucked at a fuzz on her sweater, and whispered from the side of her mouth, "Give me a minute. And we'll leave right after dinner. I promise."

"Where's the restroom?" Elise asked. Sue gave her directions to a room three doors on the left down the hall.

Quietly, Elise excused herself from the grand room and went on a search for the bathroom.

She really didn't need to, but it gave her an excuse to escape the crowd of people for a moment, and perhaps do a tiny bit of sleuthing. Her inner voice was quick to correct that. *Snooping, you mean.*

Whatever she meant, it was quiet in the hall, and tempting to open the heavy engraved doors and peek inside as she passed. *The secrets this house must keep.*

As Elise meandered the hallway, she heard raised voices. It was too quiet to hear what they were saying. Her steps faltered when she realized they were coming from what she supposed was the bathroom.

Elise paused with her hand raised to knock on the door. The voices were decidedly angry. *Do I interrupt or continue to wait?*

"You certainly look different from the last time I met you, Parker." That was Mrs. Hamilton's distinct voice.

"Perhaps it's my hair," came his accented answer.

Elise frowned. She realized she hadn't seen either of them during the family examination of the will and photograph. She looked up the hallway, realizing how it would look with her standing with her ear practically pressed to the door—like she was eavesdropping. Which, of course, she was.

The door suddenly opened, and Elise leaped back. "Oh! You scared me," she said, feigning a shaky laugh. Although the shakiness might have been more real than Elise cared to admit.

Mrs. Hamilton didn't bother to address Elise, but sidled past, leaving Parker to explain.

He shot her a pleasant smile. "So sorry about that. I was having a bit of trouble with my jacket button falling off. Unlucky, I guess. Mrs. Hamilton was having a look to see if she could fix it."

Elise couldn't help a brief look at the front of his coat where the button appeared to be in working order. She glanced back at his face.

A red flush that crept along Parker's collar seemed to be another sign he was lying.

At that moment, the butler could be heard in the other room announcing that dinner was served.

Parker excused himself, and Elise nodded. She took a moment to examine herself in the mirror before following after him.

The Christmas theme was carried into the dining room. White springs of flowers, holly, plates with gold trim, and of course the heady scent of cinnamon and vanilla.

"We're just having a light meal tonight," Ms. Christoff's tone seemed to imply the blame was squarely on Elise being an unexpected guest.

Elise took her place next to Sue. Mrs. Hamilton sat across from them. The butler efficiently served them ham, asparagus tips, and a lovely French pastry. As they were eating, Elise nudged Sue's foot.

Sue set down her fork and softly cleared her throat.

Her mom immediately looked up from the head of the table. "Susan? What are you hacking about down there?"

"I had a question. Apparently, Uncle Roger had plans to meet someone that same day as his visit to the ice rink. A detective was asking me about it. Does anyone have a clue what that was about?"

The clatter of silverware on the plates ceased as one family member looked at another.

"Well, I know what it was about," Mrs. Hamilton said. She pulled out a cigarette and lit it with a gold lighter.

"Kindly do not smoke in here," Ms. Christoff glared at her.

"Oh, I'm sorry. So sorry." She put it out in her crystal water glass and stood up. "I had a date that night with my husband. The one I'm grieving," Her eyes flashed along the table. "I'd planned to give him a watch with a private engraving. To congratulate him on being able to block the petition of the FDIC. And, really, that's all I have to say. Good night to you."

With that, she stormed from the room, with the butler chasing after her with her stole.

CHAPTER 13

"So that was how my last night went," Elise finished describing the visit to Lavina. They were in Lavina's white mustang on their way to the wedding dress boutique. Technically, Elise was on her lunch break, but Dr. Gregory had told her to take as long as she needed.

"Sue can cover for you this one time," he'd said, with Sue adamantly agreeing.

Things between Elise and Lavina were still a little stiff. Elise had gotten used to that about Lavina a long time ago, and just waited for her to process. As much as Vi would deny it, she hated confrontation with people she cared about. Elise thought it might stem from being forced to live with her grandparents at a young age. The whole "be a good girl or they won't like you" phenomenon.

So, Elise waited. Eventually Lavina would start to share, and then like an uncorked champagne bottle, she'd spill her guts.

In the meantime, Elise had a mystery on her hands. One bank manager murdered, one that was even more intriguing after meeting the family. One very dysfunctional family. Who had killed him? She thought about the suspects.

The most obvious one, at least to Elise, was this strange son showing up out of no where. His existence voided the will. Now the son got a chunk as well. But the odd way the will was written, most of the money would be funneled back into the Bank.

The amendment said anyone who contested the will would be cut from it. How enforceable was that? Elise didn't know, but she figured Ms. Christoff would get a good lawyer to find out.

Mrs. Hamilton had no motive to kill her husband. In either case, the will entitled her to the same thirty percent. Besides, it seemed she had an alibi. She was waiting at the restaurant with a gift.

There was that interesting bit of news that Grandma Babe's grandson had tried to file a petition against the bank. But since the FDIC decided not to follow through with the investigation, could she really afford to cut Michael off the suspects list? After all, he showed up into town filled with anger and more than a little craving for revenge. No matter what the reason he gave the police, he *was* at the ice rink that day.

And there was something else…what was it?

"Honestly, Elise. I don't even feel like you listen to me, anymore," Lavina said peevishly.

Elise jerked. "Oh, I'm sorry. I guess I have been a little air-headed, lately."

Lavina heaved a long sigh and flipped the car's visor down at the stop light. She dug into her purse for her lipstick and quickly patted it on. Elise was surprised Vi let that lay-up go without teasing her.

In fact, her best friend gave no response at all.

All right, I'm done waiting. "You seem kind of off, too, Lavina. What's going on with you?"

She shook her head. "It's nothing. Here we are."

Elise frowned at the denial as Lavina pulled in to the parking garage. A few minutes later, they were walking up the block.

"It's right here," Lavina said as they approached a white canopy covered door. She opened the door, and a bell trilled out.

This bridal shop was much different from the last bridal shop

Elise had once worked at. For one, there wasn't a giant poodle to greet them.

"Lavina!" a voice squealed and a woman on very tippy heels ran across the carpet toward them.

"Stella!" Lavina hugged her. The two did air kisses.

Elise stepped back, sincerely hoping she wasn't expected to air kiss. It turned out there were no kisses, but there was a lot of gushing of "Is this the bride? Oh, my goodness! She's beautiful! Just look at the bone structure!" as if she were a statue rather than an actual person standing there.

But then the champagne showed up, and after that everything was better. Elise and Lavina were soon planted in a frilly pink changing room to wait while Stella went to pull dresses for her.

Elise eyed the pink tassels on the couch.

Lavina followed her gaze. "Shh, you just ignore that. Stella is wonderful. Absolutely wonderful. She'll find something just perfect for you. I already gave her some tips."

"And I already told you I'm perfectly happy wearing my summer dress I wore to the fair."

"Elise Pepper!" Lavina's face screwed up to really give a scolding, when the curtain was whisked back. Stella stood in the doorway with a pile of white taffeta cascading out of her arms.

"Just look what I've found! A real Caroline Stacy! Just look!" The boutique owner held the dress up and the small dressing room was nearly filled with boney structures, bias tape, silk and petticoats.

Elise's mouth dropped open. Lavina's face shone with huge approval.

"Shall we try it on?" Stella asked.

"It's amazing," Elise said, her head automatically shaking no. "But it's just not me."

"Not. You?" Stella eyed Elise's simple work outfit. "I see." Her smile slipped for a moment before flashing back at a hundred watts. "Perhaps I'll keep looking, then?"

Elise breathed a sigh of relief and nodded. Stella walked out of the dressing room.

"You didn't even try that on," Lavina scolded. "It was lovely."

"Lovely for you, maybe, with that skinny figure of yours. I'd look like the abominable snowman coming down the aisle. People would run away, screaming."

Lavina's penciled eyebrow lifted at Elise's grin. She gave a quick eye roll.

"Honestly," Elise continued, just warming up, "I'd probably look like I got tangled in the living room drapes and just went with it."

A smile appeared at the corner of Lavina's mouth. She fought it.

"Tell the truth, Vi. You put her up to that, didn't you? To bring in that crazy white monstrosity!"

"Shhh! Darlin' I'd never do something like that!" Lavina whispered indignantly.

"Really. You actually liked that?"

"I think you would have looked gorgeous."

"But Vi, you know it's not me."

"I wish you would have just tried."

Stella came in again, carrying another dress. This one didn't look that much simpler than the last.

"Can you just give us a minute, please?" Elise asked gently. Stella glanced at Lavina, who nodded.

"Of course! I'll be right here, champagne in hand. Just call me when you're ready." With a swoosh, Stella closed the velvet curtain again.

Elise turned to her friend. "Come here." She patted the pink damask-covered couch. "Sit next to me."

Lavina reluctantly sat. She started to go for her purse, probably to dig for her compact.

"Wait a minute for that, Vi. Please, just tell me...Why is all this so important to you?"

Lavina pulled at the front of her shirt and glanced around the room. "It's hot in here."

Elise continued to wait.

"Oh, for heaven's sake. It's just, you deserve happiness. That fairytale princess finally finding her prince." Lavina nodded sharply at the end of her sentence, as if to say that's that.

"I don't want the fairy tale, Vi. And Brad certainly isn't perfect. But who he is, is good enough for me."

Lavina looked at her, like she had something she wanted to say. But all that came out was, "I just want to do this right for you." And then quieter, "For us."

"What do you mean, 'us'?"

Lavina studied her ring finger, her face suddenly drawn with sadness. "I don't think I'll ever have a wedding."

"What do you mean? Of course you will. You and Mr. G..."

"You don't understand. Mr. G is probably never going to

marry me." She lifted her chin a little defensively. "And that's okay."

Elise paused for a moment, needing time to consider her friend's words. "It's okay, if *you* really think it's okay. But if it bothers you, you don't have to settle. What are you feeling? Do you love him?"

"I love him. I do. But he skirts the conversation of marriage every time it's brought up. And I'm starting to realize maybe he doesn't want to marry me. So here I am, staring into the face of forty. Still with dreams of a family. Who's going to want me now?" Lavina's eyes filled with tears. As one started to fall, she angrily grabbed a tissue from her purse. "Darn it. I didn't want to cry."

"Vi...You don't stay with someone because you're afraid no one else will want you. You are worth more than that and *you* need to want you."

Elise scooted closer. "Besides, I don't think you not finding someone will ever be the problem. But you can afford to be choosy. It's not so you can find the perfect guy. It's so you can find the guy that's perfect for you."

"Perfect for me?" Lavina snorted and dabbed her face.

"Yes. Someone who makes an effort to value you and makes you want to value yourself. Someone that when you think of them, you realize they're family, they're home. The relationship can be messy, you might argue, misunderstand each other, and not always get your way. But if, in the end, you both have that respect, then it's a success."

"I'm glad you found it," Lavina said.

"Me too. And you will too. Even if it's just a new confidence in yourself. You are here on earth for a reason. You are made to be loved. One way or another, you'll find it." Elise hugged her. "And I still love you even though you tried to dress me to look like I was the wedding cake myself."

"Whatever. Simple dress, I got it. Blah, blah, blah," Lavina heaved herself to her feet. "Let's get going. I have a feeling we aren't going to find what you want here."

CHAPTER 14

*I*t turned out Elise did find something she liked as they were heading through the display room to the front door. Stella did not approve, but Lavina backed her up.

They made a quick stop at her house so that Elise could hang up the dress, carefully hiding it behind a bathrobe. Then, Lavina dropped Elise off at the chiropractic clinic and sped off, tire's squealing. Elise shook her head, but secretly was glad to see the spunky side of Lavina back.

Not that she'd admit that to her boss, who surely wouldn't appreciate the two new black tire tracks in front of his establishment.

Dr. Gregory's eyes lit up as she walked in. "Ah! Perfect

timing." He held out a blue zippered cash bag. "Can you drop this off for me? Need to get it there in time for your pay checks."

The clinic had discounts with those who paid with checks or cash. Invariably, at the end of the week, he'd have one of the girls deposit it for him. Elise definitely didn't mind the chore, especially today. She'd been meaning to visit the bank out of curiosity.

The glass door to the entrance of the bank was emblazoned with the logo of the glacier. In curly script underneath the design was the motto, just like Lucy had said. Elise silently read, "Since nearly from the ice ages, we keep you solid." The door unexpectedly opened, letting out a mom and her kid.

Elise stepped to the side to let them pass. With the blue zippered pouch tucked under her arm, she walked up to the front counter.

The bank clerk looked harried as she greeted Elise, "Welcome to Hamilton banking. How can I help you?"

Elise passed the envelope over. "Just a deposit today."

The woman brushed back a few escaping fly-aways from a bun that was slowly sliding down her head. Quickly, she ran the money through her counter. The shuffling sound of the bills always reminded Elise of walking into the hen house and hearing the chickens ruffle their wings.

"So, how are you today?" The clerk asked. Her tone indicated that she asked this a million times a day.

"I'm good. How about yourself?" Elise replied.

"It's been a long day." The clerk smiled.

Elise decided she did look rather tired. "I bet this entire week's been long, especially with..."

"Yes," the clerk nodded, knowing what Elise was referring to. "Mr. Hamilton's passing. It's been very sad and difficult." The clerk finished counting the money and printed up a slip. She slid it back over the counter, along with the empty pouch.

"I'm so sorry." Elise accepted the receipt. There was no one waiting behind her, so she felt she could expand with a question. "Was he here every day? Who's running things right now?"

"Yes. His office was upstairs. It's been a crazy few days but now our office manager is back," the clerk said. "She had to cut her vacation short, poor lady. She worked closely with Mr. Hamilton, so it's really hit her hard."

Ah, yes. The notary public who notarized the amendment to Mr. Hamilton's will. Elise nodded. "Again, I'm sorry. Hang in there, okay?"

The clerk nodded with a small smile. Elise grabbed her things and turned to go. As she walked toward the front doors, she glanced over at the personal banking center.

Here there were several glass partitions that made separate more private sections, each holding a desk and a couple chairs, for those wanting to discuss mortgages, loans, and other banking options.

A glass door at the back of the space caught her attention. She squinted to read the name, Mrs. Isobel Johnson.

"Can I help you?" One of the bank employees approached her.

"Is..." Elise hesitated, and then blurted it out, "Is Mrs. Johnson available?"

The man glanced at the office. "Let me go check."

The employee briskly walked back there and knocked on the door. Mrs. Johnson look up. The manager's face appeared drawn, with dark circles under her eyes. The specialist cracked the door to relay the message. Her gaze cut out into the lobby, meeting Elise's. With a quick nod, she gave permission for the meeting.

The employee came out. "You can go in now," he said with a smile.

Speakers overhead play Christmas music softly as Elise made

her way to the office. Mrs. Johnson had a ready smile as Elise knocked and then entered.

"Come in," she said, gesturing to the chair. "Please, sit down. How can I help you?"

Elise felt tongue-tied as she pulled out the oak chair. Mrs. Johnson leaned forward and reached for a pen. Twirling it a bit, she raised her eyebrows in a silent echo of her verbal question.

"Hi, Mrs. Johnson. I'm Elise Pepper. I'm friends with Sue Christoff."

The office manager's eyes flickered in recognition of the name.

"I was at the Hamilton house for dinner last night," Elise hedged, knowing it made her sound closer to the family than the actual truth. "They mentioned that you were close with Mr. Hamilton. When I saw you working, I guess I just wanted to know if you were okay. I-I'm the one who discovered him."

Mrs. Johnson looked away and the end of the pen found its way into her mouth. She bit the end as if needing a moment to gather her thoughts. When she glanced back, her eyes were red rimmed. They began to fill with tears.

"I'm so sorry," Elise said lamely.

Mrs. Johnson pressed her lips together in a tight, brave smile. "No, it's fine. I'm okay. I really am. I just wasn't expecting Mr. Hamilton to... but really, when is it ever expected?" She reached for a tissue from her drawer and dabbed under her eyes.

"Do you know if he had any enemies?"

She gave a sarcastic laugh. "Of course he did. Any banker does."

"Really? Why is that?"

"People get upset if they don't get approved for their loan. Or they break their contract by missing payments. Then they get upset when the bank has to enforce consequences."

"Consequences?"

"Fees. Bad credit. Repossession. Foreclosure."

"Oh, yeah," Elise nodded. "I can see what you mean."

"It's not like Mr. Hamilton wanted to. Like he wants to bring a foreclosure against someone. It's their fault." Her eyes flashed with anger.

"Right. I get that." Elise was surprised at Mrs. Johnson's vehemence. "Was there someone recent?"

"I can't tell you. It's not our policy to bring up other bank members. But, let's just say we've had a few upset customers lately. Someone actually was here the other day screaming at him. 'Someone's going to ice you, ice man,' they said. Unfortunately, one of our town's beloved businesses is not doing well."

"Grandma Babe's?"

Mrs. Johnson shrugged. "Her grandson came in for a visit. He may or may not have been the one screaming."

"I heard. Mr. Bingham brought up that the FDIC dropped the investigation."

Mrs. Johnson's face flushed. "Sounds like a person of interest, right? You'd think the police would be in here asking me questions about him."

"He threatened Mr. Hamilton?"

"I'm not at liberty to say. But Mr. Hamilton did call for security. I told him to report it to the police."

"But he didn't?"

"Mr. Hamilton was just relieved the FDIC decided to close the investigation. He didn't want to stir that all up again. Besides, he had some more exciting news on the horizon. The future was looking bright for him."

"You mean because of his son?"

Mrs. Johnson arched an eyebrow. She studied Elise carefully.

"Well, well. You certainly seem well versed in his life. Yes, that was it exactly."

"That's what happened last night," Elise said. "Mr. Bingham read the amendment to the will. You were the notary public?"

Her gaze cut away again, and she started to twirl the pen. "I'm sorry, but that's all the time I have right now. Thank you for your condolences, Ms. Pepper."

Elise stood to leave. "Thank you for your time." She turned to go.

"Oh, and Ms. Pepper?" Mrs. Johnson stopped her. "Be careful who you asked questions of. You might find yourself in a real tight place."

Elise shut the door behind her, wondering if that was meant more as a warning or as a threat.

CHAPTER 15

The rest of the day was a blur. Sue shooed her out of the office early, knowing Elise was supposed to meet Brad at Mama Mia's. But first, Elise had an after-school meeting with one of Lucy's teachers. The teacher was concerned that Lucy seemed to be more anxious than usual. Elise tried to explain the meeting that was coming up between Lucy and her mom. She made a mental note to call the teen's counselor.

So she was in a rush when she got home. Tonight was their chance to make up for their failed date night at the skating rink, and she was already late. She checked her messages on her way to the car and got a voice mail from Tamara the florist telling her that, although there weren't a lot of options this late in the game, she'd see what she could do and she'd make it beautiful.

She called her parents to make sure they'd been able to get plane tickets. Her mom wanted to chat about their new house repairs, and Elise had an agonizing few minutes of trying to sound interested while running around looking for her shoes and slipping into a dress.

She sent a text off to Lavina, thanking her again, fed Max, and threw a frozen pizza in the oven for Lucy. Then she was off for the restaurant, the one they'd planned to go to the night of ice skating.

As she parked the car, she noted Brad's jeep two stalls down.

Trying to pull herself together, she took a few cleansing breaths. And then threw all that out the window running into the restaurant.

The hostess smiled as Elise ran in. A huge potted poinsettia sat on the end of the counter. From the corner of her eye, Elise noticed a young woman in jeans and a white shirt seated on the bench normally filled with those waiting for a table.

"Hi," she said breathlessly. "I've got someone here already waiting for me."

"Are you Elise Pepper?" the hostess asked.

Elise nodded.

"Right this way."

Just as Elise turned to follow, the young woman tapped her on her arm. "Elise Pepper?"

Elise nodded again, this time confused.

The woman held out a note which caught Elise's glance. Her glance cut from it quickly up to the young woman's face.

"Here, take it." The woman pushed it toward her.

"What is this?"

"Someone just pointed you out to me and told me to give it to you."

"Someone who?" Elise looked around to see if she could catch anyone watching. The restaurant was filled with bustling people. "Who was it?"

"Look, I have to go. Can you just take it? Please?" The young woman's eyes widened in a beseeching look.

Elise reached for it. As soon as the paper touched her hand, the woman turned and ran.

"Hey! Wait!" Elise called, but there was no stopping her.

Elise studied the envelope, not at all sure she wanted to know what was inside. She tapped it against her hand.

The hostess waited expectantly. With a sigh, Elise started

after her. The waitress led her to the bar. "Your table will be ready shortly."

"Hey..." Brad said warmly as she walked up, his eyes doing that little dance up her body. He smiled. "Love your dress. You are a knock *out*."

She felt her cheeks flush, knowing she'd searched forever for this dress just for this reaction. "What? This old thing?"

He laughed. "Yeah, whatever."

Elise snuggled up to his side and let him hug her tight. After a moment, she reluctantly pulled away.

"How long were you waiting for me?" she asked.

He shrugged and took a sip of his drink. Squinting at the glass, he held it up. "About that long."

The drink was half gone. She guessed maybe fifteen minutes.

"Did you see a young lady around here?"

His eyebrow raised. "Uhhh...."

"One in a white shirt and jeans."

"I'm not looking at anyone but you." He winked.

"Brad. I'm serious. She stopped me when I came in and gave me this." Elise held out the envelope.

Brad took it. His brows lowered as he studied the front. The light was dim, but not too dim to read it. "Elise Pepper."

The bartender walked up.

"I'll have a lemon drop," Elise gave her order.

Brad handed the envelope back. "You ever see her before?"

She shook her head.

"You going to open it?" he asked.

Elise hesitated. The girl had given it to her. What if it contained something for her eyes only? *I guess that's too bad then.*

She opened it up and pulled out the note. Carefully, she smoothed the paper.

In bold print, it said: **Check out the Thunderbolts winning championship.**

The bartender brought her the drink. Elise took a quick sip and then pulled her phone from her purse.

"What are you doing?" Brad asked.

"I'm doing what the note says. Checking it out."

He sighed and finished the rest of his drink.

"What?" Elise asked. "You mad at me?"

"Well, you're late for one. And now, in the first alone time we get together, you're on your phone."

"Just hang tight. Almost done." *Come on. Come on.* The wheel was spinning. Then it came up.

Thunderbolts defeat Lexington in an epic hockey battle.

She clicked the article and turned her phone to examine the picture.

There were approximately twenty faces. She zoomed in and examined them one by one. Her breath sucked in. Without a doubt, one was very familiar.

And his name wasn't Parker.

Her voice raised in excitement as she read the name on the picture out loud, "Second-generation hockey player, Scott Daniels, shot the winning goal as the team's forward. Brad! He's not really the son. He's a fake!" Elise shoved the phone toward him.

"Wait. What?" Brad squinted and held the phone a little further away to read it. When he finished, he looked to Elise for an explanation.

"The note," she slid it over. "It says to search up the hockey winners. Well that guy right there," her finger touched on Scott's face, "is the guy I met at Sue's mother's house introducing himself as Parker. The illegitimate son of Roger Hamilton."

Brad shook his head. "How do you always get yourself right in the middle of these cases?"

"I don't know!" Elise exclaimed. "It comes naturally to me."

He narrowed his eyes at her.

She held up her hands in an innocent gesture. "I swear, I'm not searching any of this out. I just stumble into it."

"You have the best luck when it comes to stumbling," he noted dryly. He snapped a picture of the note and then forwarded the news article to his phone. After a bit more typing, he replaced his phone back in his pocket.

"What did you do?" she asked.

He grabbed a handful of peanuts from the bowl. "Sent it all to the proper authorities, the detectives on this case. So they can stumble into it." He winked at her. "Now, can we have our date?"

Just then, the hostess showed up to let them know their table was ready. Elise decided to drop it because she knew Brad really wanted this date. But all she could think about was texting Sue. *Did she know?*

CHAPTER 16

Unfortunately, Brad had to break the news to Elise that a blurry newspaper snap shot was not enough to identify Parker as Scott Daniels. "It's muddied the waters, to be sure," he admitted. "But there are a million people who look alike. And who wanted you to know this? What was their motive? Why wouldn't they have just gone to the police themselves?"

Elise had no answer for that. "Everything about this case is one step forward, two steps back," she grumbled.

Brad smiled. "It's because you take every bit of circumstantial evidence as fact. Everything has to be proven. Hang in there. We'll get our guy...or girl."

Luckily, the rest of the date was a success. Stuffed to the gills and completely relaxed for the first time in over a week, Elise had driven home to fall straight into bed. She needed to get right to sleep. Relaxing the next day wasn't in the plans. She had to get up early in order to take Lucy to visit her mom, and then that night was the school's Winter Formal.

When the alarm clock went off, Elise had been dreaming of a crazed Zamboni plowing through the backyards of her neighborhood, knocking down fences and swing sets. As silly as it was, she woke up in a sweat.

Shaking herself awake, she turned off the alarm and stared at the time. Then, with a groan, she stumbled into the bathroom for a shower.

Early morning wasn't kind to either Elise or Lucy. They both bumped around the kitchen silently while getting coffee, Elise, with her hair in a towel. Neither were morning people.

Elise dumped some food in the cat bowl, which Max promptly ignored. She took her mug to her window seat and stared outside.

There was frost in all of the window's corners. It was getting colder every day. Her little cherry tree was stripped bare of its leaves, with some stubborn cherries still hanging on like ornaments. She took a sip, musing that she needed to get a Christmas tree soon.

So much going on. So little time.

She leaned back against the cushions and mused over last night's note. If Parker wasn't who he said he was, wouldn't that be easy to prove? Just check his driver's license? Passport?

Like those can't be forged. Vi had a fake license by the time she was seventeen.

What about a plane ticket stub?

She thought some more. *But he didn't even know his dad had died. Mr. Bingham had to track him down in England to tell him.*

She groaned. *The hockey article has to be just a coincidence.*

"You ready?" Lucy asked. She was dressed in a long sweater and skinny jeans. Her face was pale, and her gray eyes looked worried.

"Yeah. Give me five minutes." Elise hurried back to her room. She pinned up her hair and found her shoes. Then they silently headed to the car.

"You all right?" she asked the teen once they had settled in the seats.

Lucy nodded, staring out the passenger window.

"It's going to be okay." Elise said, hoping it was true.

The drive was long and, except for a few switches through the radio, quiet. Elise could only imagine what Lucy was thinking about.

The tree-lined driveway of the recovery center finally appeared. Elise pulled down the driveway and parked the car. The two of them sat there— neither one of them making a move for the door. The car's engine began a slow ticking sound as it started to cool down.

"You ready?" Elise finally asked.

Lucy tucked her hair behind her ears. Elise was struck by the changing appearance of the teen. Some days, she looked so young. On others, you could clearly see the maturity in her eyes.

Her eyes looked young today. Stressed. She nodded, but it was obvious she was reluctant to get out of the car.

"I'm right here," Elise said quietly. She gave the teen a smile. "You've got this. During track season I watched you pull out all the stops on the last quarter of a race and win. Remind yourself of who you are and what you're capable of, Miss Take-no-prisoners."

Lucy snickered, and then her eyes widened as if she surprised herself with the sound. "I can do this, can't I?"

"You totally can. Your mom is on her path, and you are on yours. You're a strong, young woman."

She shot Elise a worried look and Elise felt like she could read her mind. She hurriedly continued. "I'm coming with you, though. Because even on our own two feet, sometimes we need two more feet next to us."

She grinned then. Elise cringed at the teen's poor chapped lips.

"Do you have any lip gloss?" Elise asked.

Lucy shook her head. She never carried a purse. Instead, she always jammed everything into either her pocket or her backpack.

Elise frowned and dug through her purse. She found some chapstick. "Here, use this."

Lucy smoothed it on. She started to hand it back when Elise said, "Keep it. You might need it later."

Now, there was no more stalling. "You ready?"

Lucy nodded and jerked the car door open. She climbed out, with Elise following on the other side. Elise grabbed her purse and then brushed her hair off her shoulder. Her stomach jumped with nervousness. *Don't freak out. You're the adult here.*

The two of them walked through the parking lot scattered with pinecones and leaves. Near the sidewalk, the leaves had gathered in wet piles. The smell reminded Elise of winter walks with her dad through the woods. A deep, mouldering smell.

The building in the distance appeared innocent. Christmas lights hung from the bordering trees. Snowflake decals decorated the windows.

This place has helped heal a lot of people.

Elise sincerely hoped Lucy's mom was one of those people.

They walked to the doors, and Elise opened one. Inside was painted in a light soothing green, with couches and chairs scattered in the common area, along with tables covered in books and magazines.

There was a receptionist and what appeared to be a check-in desk. Elise walked over, with Lucy a few steps behind.

"Hi," Elise said as the receptionist gave her a welcoming grin. "We're here to see—"

"Mom?" Lucy interrupted.

Elise turned to look. A thin woman stood up from a chair at the far end of the room, next to a window. The window's light glowed around her, making her appear even frailer. Elise couldn't make out the face.

Lucy had already left her side and was hurrying across the room.

The woman stood like a statue.

Elise's heart squeezed. *Lift your arms. Say something! This is your daughter!*

Lucy stopped short before the woman. They stared at each other for a moment. They were nearly the same size. Slowly, Lucy wrapped her mom in a hug.

Elise started forward. Indignity was building inside of her. *You hug your daughter!* As she got closer, she saw she'd misunderstood.

Tears poured out of Lucy's mom's eyes. Her mouth was stiff with a silent cry. She was a picture of agony, shame. Gratitude. She dipped her chin down until her forehead rested beside her daughter's. Carefully, she tucked one arm around Lucy, and then the other. They clung to each other, both of them quaking.

Finally, Lucy's mom straightened up. A hint of a smile curved her pale lips as she brushed the hair back from her daughter's shoulders. "I like what you did with your hair."

Lucy's face shone in a way that Elise had never seen before. "You noticed? I chopped it all off."

Her mom chuckled. "I can see that. And now I can see your

face better. And it's so beautiful." The mom's bottom lip quivered. Elise could feel her own throat tightening.

"How are you doing?" Lucy asked her mom.

"I'm good. One day at a time." Suddenly her mom was shuffling through her pockets. She pulled out a token. "Look! Ninety days."

Lucy took the token and hummed in admiration. "Great job, Mom."

"More importantly, how are you?"

"I'm good. I'm doing real good. I have a job."

"Really!" her mom smiled. "And how's school?"

"School? We're really going to start with that?" Lucy made a face.

Her mom laughed again, thin and papery. "No. I guess we better not. Actually, there's some stuff I've been wanting to tell you." Her eyes caught her daughter's. "But I'd like to talk privately."

At those words, Elise slowly backed away. Lucy was fine. She didn't need her, now.

The mom reached for her daughter's hand. "Want to take a walk?"

Together, they headed out the front door.

Lucy never looked back, having forgotten about Elise. Even though Elise expected that, she didn't expect the stab of pain. She shook her head as if she could shake the feeling away, chastising herself for being silly.

For them to be reunited was always the plan.

She just never expected to love the girl so much, herself.

Sighing, Elise walked out to her car to give them space. Sitting in the driver's seat, the car's silence that had been bearable on the way here was suddenly thunderous. She flipped on the radio and searched through the stations, eventually settling on one. To distract herself even more, she started a note on her phone.

Claudia seemed surprised when she met Parker. Can I find out why?

Did the siblings benefit from their brother's death? I'd say yes, with the old will. But not with the son in the picture.

Claudia benefited.

What about Grandma Babe? She couldn't possibly be involved. Or could she?

And what on earth are we going to eat at the wedding reception?

Elise glanced at the go-fund-me and was pleased to see it was at eight thousand. Yesterday, the student government had placed flyers all around town. *Lucy was a part of that.* She glanced out into the lawn and saw Lucy with her mother, both of them smiling.

She's going to be okay.

CHAPTER 17

*I*t had been a long day at the recovery center, and tonight was the Winter Formal. Elise pulled the brush through Lucy's hair, marveling at how the light shone off of it. Silky. Beautiful. So different from when Elise first met her hiding down an alley, alone and scared.

"You're beautiful, Lucy. Inside and out."

Lucy rolled her eyes. "Elise, that's so corny." But she smiled, and Elise knew she loved it.

"Smart. Caring. Funny." Elise added.

"Yeah, yeah, yeah." Lucy said. Her cheeks turned slightly pink.

Elise spun Lucy around on the stool so she was facing her. A lump started growing in her throat and she tried to smile. That darn smile made her eyes water. "I'm so proud of you. You did great today. You have become my hero."

Lucy's eyes looked suspiciously misty themselves. The two women hugged tightly for a second, and then both pushed away to try to get a grip on their emotions.

"So, I think for this occasion, we should use my gold eyeshadow pallet. What do you think?" Elise asked Lucy in the mirror.

Lucy bit her lip and stared down at the floor.

"What?" No answer. "Lucy?"

"I, um, I might have borrowed it."

Elise raised her eyebrow.

"I'll be right back!" The teen scooted off the stool and ran to her room.

She was back in a flash, and soon she had Lucy's make up finished. Then Elise started working on herself. Both she and Brad were going to the dance as chaperones. She had to admit she was kind of excited.

She went to look for her shoes and discovered those were missing as well. After yelling for Lucy to find them—and

Lucy repeating, "I'm sorry! Sorry!"—she sat on the bed to wait.

While she waited, Elise grabbed her phone and searched up the Go-Fund-Me for Grandma Babe. The school had graciously offered a quarter of the proceeds of the ticket sales to the charity. Still, even with that huge lump sum, they were still quite a bit short. The total was twenty-two thousand dollars.

Biting her lip, she exited out of the browser. Just as she was about to set the phone down, she noticed an unread text. She clicked it to see from Lavina,—**Save your pennies because I have a feeling there's going to be a ton of baby showers in nine months because of that power outage! Sarah Jane just messaged me that she's pregnant!**

Elise chuckled at Lavina's prediction of Angel Lake's population exploding do to the power outage. Too bad it knocked out the cameras at the rink. She was about to respond when Lucy yelled for her.

"Come out here! Hurry! Look what just pulled up!" Lucy squealed from the window seat. Elise hurried from her room and over to the seat, nudging Max out of the way to see.

A white stretch HumVee parked in the driveway.

"What the heck?" Elise said, pulling back the curtain even further to get a good look.

"It's Brad!" Lucy squealed even louder. She bounced off the seat to run toward the door, dress held high, and tottering on her heels like she was a little girl in her Momma's shoes.

The doorbell rang just as Lucy flung open the door.

Brad stood there with a bouquet of white roses. In the center was one single red, which he plucked out.

"Your chariot awaits. These are for you." He handed the bouquet to Lucy. "You look lovely."

Lucy's excited pitches reached even higher, making Brad grin. She sprang off for the kitchen with her flowers.

Brad turned and slowly meandered toward Elise, his eyes doing a slow sweep. "What are you even doing to me? You're so beautiful."

He slowly kissed her and then handed her the single red rose. "For *my* rose."

Elise dipped her head to breathe in its scent. "I love you."

He took her hand. "I love you more."

THE WINTER FORMAL WAS ADORABLE, at least to Elise, not that she would ever dare utter that word. These kids were so proud of the work they'd done decorating, and Elise was impressed.

Mistletoe hung from the doorways and white and blue silk curtains covered the walls. Crystals to mimic ice hung from every available surface of the gym. Even the air glittered from the strobe lights flashing on the silver confetti in the air. Fresh white flowers cascaded from huge floor vases. Around the edges of the room, circular tables sparkled with silver and white cloth, ribbons and snowflakes. And on every table, as well as a huge display at the entrance, was an embossed picture of Grandma Babe's restaurant.

Elise picked up one of the cards to see the words, "In honor of Grandma Babe. Let's save the peach pie!"

So cute. The music, on the other hand, was loud and pounding. Elise grimaced as the DJ cranked it up. "I must be crazy to be here."

"What?" Brad asked, looking down at her.

"I said, I'm officially an old lady."

Brad laughed and tucked her in close. "And I have a crush on the dance's chaperone. Never thought that day would happen," he admitted. He laughed again at the face she made. "Come on, kid. Let's dance."

Elise looked around as Brad led her to the dance floor. She was tickled to see Grandma Babe, dressed in a long purple gown, dancing with one of the guys, a football player judging by the size of him. The teen twirled her around and she had a grin from ear to ear. She nudged Brad to have a look, and they both watched, smiling.

Soon there was a circle around Grandma Babe and her partner. The audience started clapping and cheering, which only egged Grandma Babe and her partner on. The two of them twirled, hopped and swung. At the end of the song, he dipped her.

Everyone applauded with loud whoops. Grandma Babe's face was flushed and full of hilarity as he pulled her back up.

Elise clapped until her hands hurt. She glanced around at the dancer's cheering fans. And caught the glance of someone standing in the crowd she didn't expect to see.

Grandma Babe's grandson.

He was easy to spot because he was the only one not smiling.

"Brad," Elise said, tugging on him, trying to get his attention. But it was too loud and crazy for him to notice. By the time he glanced in her direction, the grandson had melted back into the crowd.

As the evening wore on, Elise danced until she thought her

feet would fall off. Every time she looked for Lucy, the teen always seemed to be having fun, either talking animatedly with friends, or dancing with laughter in her eyes.

Then it was time to announce the Winter Dance Royalty. Everyone screamed when Grandma Babe was crowned Queen, with her football dance partner the King.

The DJ called for the last dance and Elise couldn't help but be relieved it was almost over. She found Brad again. "What do we do about Lucy?"

"Do?" he asked, looking for the teen.

"Yeah. Do we take her home now? She wants to go hit Dennys with her friends."

He hugged her. "She was on her own before you met her. She can handle this. Let her go."

"Oh, my gosh! You make me sound like a helicopter mom!"

"Aren't you?" he asked, one eyebrow raised.

She shook her head and went to search for Lucy. She didn't see her in the gym, so she headed out to hallway—breaking up two couples along the way—before starting for the bathrooms. There she found Lucy fixing her makeup and talking with her two best friends.

"Home by one?" Elise asked.

Lucy rolled her eyes, but said, "Okay."

"I'll see you later. Be safe and have fun," Elise said.

Lucy waved before turning back to her friends.

Along the way back to Brad, she passed a short hallway filled with lockers. She glanced down it just to be sure everything was okay, and stopped short to see Grandma Babe and her grandson.

Grandma Babe's crown sat crooked on her head, and her smile was long gone.

Elise paused to listen. Yes, she was snooping. But technically, that was her job tonight, right?

Her spine stiffened as she heard Grandma Babe angrily, and with more than a trace of fear, say, "I can't believe you did that, Michael. The restaurant wasn't worth this. What if you get caught?"

CHAPTER 18

*E*lise stood just out of sight at the entrance of the hallway.

"Shh!" Michael said furiously. "We'll talk about this later."

"Later? They're throwing this dance in my honor! What if these people find out?"

"Grandma, I did what I had to do. Now I've got to go. You coming or what?"

Their voices started getting closer. Elise panicked. She turned around and headed as fast as she could in the other direction before realizing that wouldn't work. Reluctantly, she turned back. Walking briskly, like she'd come from far away, she hit the hallway entrance just as they were coming out.

Their eyes both widened in surprise when they saw her.

"Hi, guys!" Elise said cheerfully. "You having fun?"

Michael immediately scowled and glanced away. Grandma Babe's mouth moved soundlessly for a bit, showing she was flustered. But she got back on solid ground and reached for the tiara perched on her snowy white hair. "Any day I get named queen is a good day," she said, straightening the crown.

"You bet it is!" Elise laughed, continuing toward the gym. "I'm looking for Brad. You seen him? No? Well, you two have a good night."

"You too, missy!" Grandma Babe called after her. There was no response from Michael.

Elise hurried into the emptying gymnasium. A few other chaperones were herding the kids out like chickens from the scrap heap.

She reached for Brad's arm. His welcoming smile disappeared when he saw the expression on her face. "What's wrong?"

"We need to get out of here. I know who did it!"

"Did what?" he asked. His face started to take on the patient look that drove Elise nuts.

"Come on. Let's go outside. Hurry!"

He glanced around and caught another chaperone's eye. "We okay to go?"

The chaperone gave him a thumbs up, and the two of them headed outside.

Elise shivered as the cold air bit through her thin dress. It felt like it might snow again. Brad shrugged his jacket off and placed it around her shoulders.

"What's going on with you?" he asked, giving her back a rub. "You came flying into the gym like you just found out the house was on fire."

She glanced around the parking lot. It was mostly empty, with a few stragglers whooping it up outside various limousines and other rentals. A couple chaperones were standing about, making sure there wasn't any trouble.

But she didn't see Grandma Babe or Michael.

"Geez, what are you looking for?" Brad muttered, giving the lot a quick study. After not seeing anything out of the ordinary, he stared back at her.

"Just get me to the car and I'll tell you," she whispered, picking up her pace. Her breath came out in white puffs. Goosebumps trickled down her arms and she crossed them under the jacket.

The HumVee was waiting for them. The driver opened the door, and Brad gave her a hand up into the seat, which was difficult to navigate in her tight dress and heels. After she situated herself, he hurried around and climbed into the other side.

"Now," he said turning toward her. "What's this all about." His eyes immediately cut across the parking lot again, casing it.

"You're not going to believe this, but I heard them. I heard Grandma Babe and her grandson arguing down the hall. And her grandson was confessing!" Her words sputtered out in one long run-on sentence in Elise's excitement.

Brad raised his eyebrows. "Whoa. Confessed what, exactly?"

Elise opened her mouth to answer. The words froze in her throat. What *was* he confessing? As she tried to answer, her well-formed idea started to slip away. "Well... I don't know, exactly."

"You don't know?" He waited patiently.

The driver started the HumVee and shifted to drive. The SUV jerked forward as the driver took his foot off the brake.

"Brad! You don't understand. Michael said he had to do it to save the restaurant! He had the perfect motive to kill Hamilton. Revenge!"

He nodded, slowly. "I believe you. That really sounds bad. But do *what* exactly? For all we know, he put out ads all over Craigslist as Skipper the Stripper, with the proceeds going to pay off the foreclosure."

Elise groaned and covered her face.

"I'm sorry, honey." Brad's voice lowered in sympathy. "I know this is driving you crazy. You going to have to trust the detectives to do their work."

"I do trust them. It's just to hear him say that and then hear how mad and scared Grandma Babe sounded...." Her words trailed off.

"I'll tell the team to give Michael another look again. But, I need to be honest with you. He's way down on the list of suspects."

"Are you serious? How can that be possible? He was right at the ice rink when it happened." Elise was aghast.

"Simple law of physics."

"What are you talking about?"

"The blow came from someone left-handed."

"Well, lovely. I guess that narrows it down," Elise said with a sigh. "To what, a billion people?"

"Well, it narrows him out, anyway. Unfortunately."

"There's no way you could fake it?" Elise asked. "Fake being left-handed to throw people off?"

Brad shook his head. "Nope. Not with a blow like that. It needs a certain angle with the force. It wouldn't happen naturally for someone right-handed."

Elise settled back in the seat with her arms crossed. Yes, she felt like pouting. She'd been so positive she had the murder suspect.

She bit her thumbnail, brain still spinning. *What could Michael have meant, then?*

"Don't worry too much about it," Brad reached over and gave Elise's knee a squeeze. "We'll get 'em."

She stared glumly out the window. The oncoming traffic had dwindled at this time of night to just occasional headlights flashing by. After a moment, she pulled out her phone. Her signal wasn't great, but she managed to search up Grandma Babe's Go-Fund-Me.

Her mouth dropped open. A chill ran down her spine.

The total was one hundred and two thousand dollars. Elise scrolled through the list of donations, mostly all between ten and fifty dollars.

There it was. The last one. Eighty thousand dollars from one donor.

The donor's name was Anonymous.

CHAPTER 19

"*B*rad!" she shrieked.

Brad gave a startled yell. He was instantly defensive. "Geez Louise, lady! You're going to kill me scaring me like that!" He rolled his shoulders, trying to relax.

"I'm sorry. I'm sorry. I didn't mean to scare you. It's just that there's been a donation to Grandma Babe's Go-Fund-Me. An anonymous donation! In the amount of eighty thousand dollars."

"Are you serious?" he asked. "This case gets more and more interesting."

"Right! So maybe Michael did do something after all!" Elise sat back, arms crossed before her, feeling vindicated.

Brad chuckled softly.

Elise looked at him in surprise. "What?"

"There you go, leaping to conclusions again. Elise, you can't just decide how to read the facts. They have to prove themselves. You don't know who made the donation. You don't know why. And, technically, there's nothing illegal about it."

"Can you guys contact Go-Fund-Me about it?"

"That will take a court order. If it warrants it, we'll get it done."

Elise rolled her head against the back of the seat with a groan. "I could never be a detective. Too many ups and downs."

Brad laughed again. "Look, I'll give you something to whet your appetite. We tracked down the ice-skate."

"Yeah?" Elise looked over interested.

"It was a vintage 1975 Super Tacks hockey skate. Super heavy. Perfect for breaking a neck."

Elise shivered and rubbed the back of her neck. "That's gruesome. But it's a good clue. Now where did it come from?"

Street lights flashed against Brad's face. He shrugged. "You can find them on eBay."

Elise groaned and flopped back against the seat.

"The real news is that it was a goalie skate. Which makes sense because it's the heaviest they made."

"So we have the skate, the note to me, and now the anonymous donation. We have what might be a forged genealogy and a fake son, and a crumbled note that turned out to be a date for the gift of a new pocket watch. Yet, at the time he was supposed to show up to meet his wife at the restaurant, he went to the ice skating rink. None of this makes any sense."

"And that's why I like investigating," Brad said with a smile. "Really makes you think. It's like the ultimate puzzle."

"A puzzle that includes the pieces of people's ruined lives."

"Yeah, but the sweet taste of victory when I can put the scum bag behind bars. Makes it all worth it."

ELISE WENT to bed that night, still trying to sort through everything. She tossed and turned well past the point when Lucy returned home and tiptoed to her own bedroom.

Finally, she gave up. There was no point in trying to force sleep if it wasn't going to come. She wandered out to the kitchen with Max at her feet. Even in the middle of the night, the cat was loyal enough to stick with her anywhere.

Either that or he wanted food.

She got down a mug and scooped in some hot chocolate powder. After adding water, she gave it a stir and set it in the microwave.

There was something missing. Something obvious.

At the ding of the machine, she brought the drink over to the table and opened up her computer. Max rubbed against her ankles, so she scooped him on her lap. Leaning forward, she searched for the hockey championship again.

There he was. Scott Daniels. She zoomed in on the picture. It might just be a crappy black-and-white photo, but that was him. The coal-black hair. She knew it.

She took a sip of cocoa. There had to be other pictures. She tried Google, but the name only brought up the news article. It was a dead end.

"Who is this kid, Max?" She stroked the cat's head, and he contentedly purred. There was something about the article. Something that was really bugging her. She almost had it....

"What are you doing up?" Lucy yawned almost in her ear.

Elise screamed, causing Max to leap from her lap, fur flying.

"Oh, I'm sorry. I heard some rattling around in here." Lucy looked horrified until the hilarity of Elise's reaction struck her. She started laughing so hard she had to grab the counter for balance.

Max looked haughtily out from under the kitchen table. He turned his back to them and began licking his fur.

"Whatever, Chuckles. Did you have fun tonight?"

"Yeah," Lucy poured a glass of water and turned to bring it back to her room. "Well, I'm going to be going now. It was nice scaring you."

"Whatever. Goodnight, you little turkey."

Elise listened for Lucy's door to close and then started her search again. Just go back to the beginning. She brought up the article and read it, this time out loud, hoping the clue would jump out at her. "Second-generation Thunderbolt champion hockey player, Scott Daniels shot the winning goal as the team's forward."

Wait, was that it? Could it be? After typing a few minutes, she ended up at the school's archives. She searched year by year through the hockey pictures. Nothing came up. She rubbed her eyes.

Hang on a second, didn't it say 'champions?'

She went back to Google and searched for the Thunderbolt

Championships. It brought up the first link that she had clicked on. This time she scrolled further down the list.

The school had won the state championship three more times. The first, five years earlier. The second twelve years earlier, and the third, sixteen years earlier.

She was surprised there weren't any older ones. But, with her heart pounding, she clicked on the last one.

Quickly, she scanned through the names. She was in near shock at the end of the list. Disappointment hit her like an avalanche of mud. She'd been *so* sure!

There was no one on the team with the last name of Daniels. That put that theory to dust.

She was just about to close the computer and call it a night when another thought hit. Slowly, she scanned through the old champion players again, this time studying the pictures. She was hardly breathing as she found the position of Goalie.

Next to it was a name that made her blood run cold.

CHAPTER 20

*E*lise could hardly sleep that night. But she remembered what Brad had said, and struggled hard not to jump to conclusions. She had a few more things to search before she was ready to bring this all up to Brad again.

She'd been thinking a lot lately on how Brad mentioned that the power outage had helped the murderer. At the very least, it had blown the ancient cameras at the ice rink.

But it did open up the possibility for something else. Was there any way the power outage helped *them*? Carefully, she'd been raking over her memories of the last week, trying to think of anything she could have missed. And, an idea had occurred to her.

Elise pulled into the grocery store and parked. This was it.

This could make it or break it for her. She tapped nervously on the steering wheel before grabbing her purse and climbing out.

The store was empty this Sunday morning, with most people sleeping in or at church. Christmas music was being piped through the store speakers, and there were new displays of wrapping paper and tape on the aisle end caps. Green garland looped around a pyramid stack of half-racks of soda to imitate a Christmas tree.

Annie was working again, to Elise's relief. Today, the older woman's blonde hair was pinned back in two lopsided pigtails. She still wore the Christmas ornament name tag, but it was looking a little worse for wear. One of the ornaments had fallen off.

Elise stood in her lane.

"You don't have anything to buy?" The cashier asked. She snapped her gum, one hand on her hip like she didn't have time for any funny business.

"I just have a quick question." Elise gave her most disarming grin. "It will just take a second of your time."

"And what's that, chickee?"

"Is there any way I could see the receipts from a couple of days ago?"

"Why?" Her eyes narrowed. "You've got something juicy?"

"I'm looking for someone specific. The power was out, remember? Everyone had to sign their name. You mentioned a funny looking signature. Can you look for this one?" Elise wrote the name out on a piece of paper. "Here. Take my phone with you. If you find it, can you take a picture of it?"

The cashier studied the name, her tongue slowly tracking along her bottom lip. Finally, she crumpled the paper in her fist. "What's it worth to you?"

"Twe....fifff... How about a hundred dollars?" Elise changed her price at Annie's finger waggling upwards.

"You got it." Annie plunked a closed sign at the end of her conveyer belt. She shooed the other customers over. "Next line, please. Move to the next line. Hey, Nancy!" she called to the cashier on her left. "I'm going on my break."

Elise's eyebrows rose. She couldn't believe how bold Annie was. And, apparently neither could the two people behind her who huffed as they moved their baskets over to Nancy's line.

But she was thankful.

———

It took Annie much longer than Elise thought it would,

about forty minutes. During that time, Elise browsed through all the magazines in the racks, checked out the flower bouquets, and eyed the deli where the delicious smells of fried chicken made her stomach growl as they stocked up for the Sunday lunch crowd.

Finally, Annie appeared. She shuffled from the back room like her feet hurt. One of her pigtails was even more crooked if that were possible.

"Here you go," she said, trying to catch her breath. "I hope that's what you wanted. He came in a few times during those two days, so I snapped all of them."

"Thank you so much!" Elise exclaimed.

"Now," Annie held out her hand. "Where's my money?"

"Right." Elise looked around and snagged a bouquet of flowers. "I just need some change back."

Once the exchange was done, Elise ran to her car. She could hardly wait to look at the photos. She opened the first one.

Annie had done a good job. The signature was focused crisp and clean. And in a very clear left handed slant.

She remembered the last time she'd seen this handwriting. It gave her chills to know that she'd been that close to a cold-blooded murderer.

Her hands were shaking as she dialed Brad. *Come on. Pick up. Pick up. Pick up.*

"I've got thirty seconds, so make it quick," he said as he answered.

"Do you guys still have the note that Mrs. Hamilton said she gave her husband?"

"Of course. We don't lose clues."

"Well, I have a signature I want you to compare against it."

"Really?" he said. He chuckled softly. "I should have known."

"I'm serious, Brad. This time I really know who did it."

"Meet you at the deli in an hour. Bring your evidence. If you're right, I'll buy you lunch."

"Pish," Elise said. "If I'm right, I want a honeymoon. You have to pick a hotel because I need to get out of here."

"Mmhmm. I like this bet and I'm praying you're right."

AN HOUR LATER, Elise parked her car down the street from Sweet Sandwiches Deli, Lavina's own personal business. Every parking spot in front of the cute deli had already been taken, and the tables outside were filled.

Her phone dinged with a message, and she fished it out to read it before going in.

It was from Sue. **—So I have something to say and you're not going to be happy with me. It was me who sent you that note. You said you were meeting Brad, so I got one of my friends (we were together in the Peace Corps). Anyway, she brought it to you. Something seemed weird about Parker. But I feel like a heel, and I don't want to get anyone into trouble. He just looked familiar to me. And I remember this specific hockey game (our school was the one who played his.) I was hoping if I sent it anonymously, maybe you'd poke around. See if I was crazy or not. Anyway, this guilt is the pits, and I had to confess. I hope you forgive me. Sue**

Elise felt her jaw drop as she read it. She'd forgotten that Sue and Parker were about the same age. That made sense she would have seen him as a teenager when her school played his.

Wow. I never would have guessed. She wanted to keep her response back simple. Since she hadn't even talked to Brad yet about what she was learning, she definitely didn't want to talk with Sue about it. After all, this was Sue's family that was involved. It could put Sue in a difficult spot, and Elise didn't want to accidentally give anyone a heads up while the police were still investigating.

Elise answered—**Of course I'm not mad, but I'm glad you let me know it was you. That was a little freaky. We'll talk later.**

After pressing send, Elise walked inside the deli. Dan, one of Lavina's employees, was behind the counter. He was taking someone's order, but his eyes lit up as he saw her enter.

"Hey, Elise! Lavina's waiting for you in the back room."

Well, Elise had to admit, she felt like royalty skipping past the long line and sidling behind the counter. She felt the eyes on her, wondering who *she* was, and why she got the special privilege.

Lavina was indeed waiting for her in the small break room. She had two glasses of sweet tea and a plate of macaroons waiting for her.

"Hey! This is fun!" Elise said as she sat down. "Your favorite cookies!"

"Brad called to let me know y'all were swinging by. He said you had some news about the case. Well, you can smack me with a fish before I let you spread some juicy gossip around with me not there."

Elise laughed.

Brad showed up just then, poking his head around the corner. He wore his police uniform, and his hair was sticking up in several places. Elise leaned over to smooth it back as he sat down.

"Hard day?" she asked.

"Better now," he smiled back.

"All right, you two. Save your love dove stuff for when people with sensitive stomachs aren't around. Spill your guts, Elise."

Elise opened her phone and found the first picture. She passed it to Brad. "Scroll to the right."

He studied the first picture and zoomed in. A low whistle came from his mouth. "You've got to be kidding me."

Lavina bobbed up to look over his shoulder. Her brow wrinkled. "Henry Bingham. So what?"

The final shot was one she'd taken the night before showing the High School roster of hockey players. She'd zoomed into one name and snapped the picture. Thunderbolts Goalie— Henry Bingham. And on his wrist that held a hockey stick was a black tattoo.

Brad gave an incredulous laugh. "All right, Columbo. I've got to hear this. How'd you figure it out?"

Just then, Dan showed up with a plate of sandwiches. "You

said to bring them after the officer showed up?" he said with a little uncertainty to Lavina.

"That's great, just set them here." Lavina directed to the center of the table.

Brad picked one up and took a bite. "Go on. I'm listening."

Elise took a deep breath. "You told me not to look at the circumstantial evidence, but I sort of had to. There were a lot of tiny clues. At first everyone seemed like a suspect, especially Michael. But when I pulled away, and looked at the clues one by one, I came up with a different picture."

"Keep going."

"So, one thing that kept coming back to me was how much Henry Bingham had his finger in everything. In fact, Claudia mentioned that the lawyer was the one who'd introduced her to her husband. It was based on Mr. Bingham's word that he received a letter from some solicitor in East Sussex. He was the one that brought Parker into the picture. And he did it in a way that would make Parker seem innocent as well, by making all contact be between two lawyers, and even being the one to let Parker know that his father had died."

"So, is Parker actually Roger Hamilton's son or not?" Lavina asked.

Elise took a sip of sweet tea and waited to drop the news. "He's not. He's actually Henry Bingham's son."

"What in the world?" Lavina exclaimed.

"Crazy, right? Scott is the illegitimate child Henry had when he was a teenager. With his family running the big Bingham law firm, they managed to keep it hush hush for a long time. But someone knew. Because when the son went on to follow his dad's hockey footsteps years later, someone mentioned that he was a 2nd generation winner in the article. I searched, and that was the farthest back that the Thunderbolts had won."

"Who's the mom?"

"Someone with the maiden name of Daniels. And I have my suspicions, but no hard proof yet." She winked at Brad.

"Claudia," he said.

"Why, detective! Are you making snap conclusions without the proper evidence?"

"Ha, ha," he said dryly, forwarding all the photos from her phone to his. "She was probably the only one to be able to get the private photo of the girl with Hamilton."

"And Bingham wrote on it to use as evidence with his amazing left-handed handwriting," Elise added.

"So that's where the goalie skate came from. It was his," Brad said thoughtfully.

"But why?" Lavina asked. "What on earth was his motive?"

"With the change in the will, the majority of Hamilton's estate is now funneled back into the banking company. Bingham is the executer and overseer. He can draw a salary, create financial folders and investments, and open off shore accounts. And with his real son as the inheritor, they controlled the entire company."

"And with Claudia's share, they manage to bilk almost his entire estate. That's why he provided an alibi for her by putting that note in Hamilton's pocket after he killed him." Brad continued to type. "I'm sending all of this to the lead detective in the case. He'll get this sorted out. I'm confident there's enough here to get an arrest warrant. I told you we always get the bad guy."

"But not without some help from our Elise," Lavina raised a penciled in eyebrow. "She's one smart cookie. Speaking of cookies," she picked up a macaroon. "Aren't these delish?"

CHAPTER 21

The next week or so passed like they always do when there is never enough time to get everything done. There were wedding preparations to make, invites to get out, and the last few details of the murder to solve.

Mr. Bingham was indicted on charges of first degree murder. His son, Scott Daniels, was indicted on charges of committing fraud. The plan began a few years back when Mr. Bingham's father passed the Hamilton contract to his son, Henry. Henry had read Hamilton's will and slowly began to scheme.

It turned out that Claudia had been Henry's high school sweetheart all those years ago. He'd negotiated an intro between her and Roger Hamilton, telling her that if she played her cards right, she'd be set for life.

Claudia insisted that she didn't understand what "play your cards right" meant, other than to be a good, dutiful wife. Elise heard that she'd emphasized the last words a few times during the police interview.

Slowly, Bingham had begun the introduction of Scott, or Parker Hamilton, the name on his false ID. By the time the falsified records of the blood test came through, Roger Hamilton was sold. It took very little persuasion on Bingham's part to convince Hamilton to change his will.

Then the die was cast for when Bingham was ready to strike. But when the FDIC contemplated an investigation into the loan practices of the Hamilton bank, Bingham had panicked. He'd drawn up more than a few of the shady contracts.

Bingham had lured Hamilton to the ice rink under the guise of meeting his son. Bingham had chosen that place because it was well known that Michael had screamed, "Someone's going to ice you, ice man!"

When it became public knowledge that Bingham was arrested, Michael came forward, citing himself as a witness to the crime. He'd seen it happen when he went down for an interview. When asked why he didn't come forward when the body was found, he stated that been too terrified to accuse Bingham.

Bingham contested that statement, saying Michael had tried

to extort him for money in exchange for his silence. Michael denied it.

Elise wasn't sure Bingham was lying. She remembered the conversation between Grandma Babe and Michael at the high school dance.

Well, she may never know all the answers, but things seemed to have been wrapped up pretty well. Elise glanced at herself in the mirror, before picking up her earrings. A set of diamond studs, just for today's occasion. Slowly, she put them in her ears.

It was time to clear her mind. Think of something else.

Today was her wedding day.

"You ready? We don't want to be late." Elise's mom placed her hands gently on Elise's shoulders and smiled in the mirror at her.

"I can't believe I'm doing this again," Elise whispered. Butterflies crashed like jousting combatants in her stomach.

"You sure you want to do it? I never asked the first time, but I'm asking now."

Elise looked at her ring—a delicate rose diamond with two emerald slivers for leaves. Brad's sweet face came into her mind. The way he'd put it on her finger and then entwined his fingers through hers. The way he'd kissed her, how connected she'd felt.

She'd never felt that way before.

"Definitely," she said, giving the ring a spin with her thumb. She stood up and studied herself in the mirror. Lavina had won out and Elise wasn't wearing her summer dress after all. Instead, she had on the silk sheath that had turned up the nose of the boutique owner. But she loved it, and ran her palms down it now. It wasn't white, but a deep bronze. She'd worn white once and wanted something fresh for this time. The color contrasted in the most heavenly way against her skin, bringing out the sun-burnished peach of her cheeks, and highlighting the gold flecks in her eyes.

Her mother had worked on her hair—no easy task—and it was pinned and sprayed to a near inch of its life. But, as long as you didn't touch it, it appeared soft and shiny in an elegant updo with small sprays of white flowers tucked in the waves.

Lavina was in the living room, waiting for her. She'd wanted to give Elise a moment of privacy with her mom. That thoughtfulness pierced Elise's heart. Knowing Lavina didn't have a mom made her gesture all the more heartbreaking.

Lucy was already at the gazebo with Brad. Elise glanced at the clock.

"Yes," her mom said softly. "It's time." She turned her

daughter to look at her and searched her eyes. Finally, she smiled. "I can see you're ready. This is what you want. You've grown so much from my little girl, to an uncertain young woman, to this confident, amazing, mature woman before me now. I'm so proud of you."

Oh no. The lump was growing in her throat and her eyes were starting to feel suspiciously blurry. "Mom," she croaked.

"Yes, dear?"

"I think you just called me old."

"What? I never—"

They both burst into laughter. The tears came anyway, but it was much easier to endure.

With a final wipe under her eyes, her mom hugged her and headed from the room. Lavina poked her head in.

"My goodness, you look lovely. Quite a contrast from that crazy laughter I heard a minute ago. I was afraid a flock of loons had committed a siege against this room."

Elise smiled. "It was just my mom complimenting me."

Lavina arched an eyebrow and then checked her lipstick in the mirror. "Before we go, I have something to tell you."

"What?" Elise asked.

"Promise you won't say a word?"

Elise rolled her eyes.

"I'm sorry, I'm sorry." Lavina held her hands up. "I know better. Anyway, I've just become a twenty-five percent shareholder in a brand new restaurant."

A shiver ran up Elise's back. Like a flash, it came to her what her friend was going to say next. "You're telling me..."

Lavina nodded. "Yep. You know how I've always loved pie. I'm the anonymous donation to Grandma Babe's restaurant. She's given me twenty-five percent ownership in the business. We're thinking about collaborating together on a new catering business!"

Elise smiled. "Vi, that's wonderful. What made you decide to do that?"

"You know, I got to thinking. I've had a privileged life. You know I'm adventurous. But I've kind of just been focused on myself. I figured it might be nice to invest in something important. Maybe something a little outside of my comfort zone. But still something I love."

"You're the skinniest woman I know who loves food this much."

"You know it, darlin'. Anyway, I have a lot of money now. I

can give back. Besides, it would be good for me to have a project like starting a catering company to sink my teeth into. I might need a little distracting."

Lavina glanced at Elise again, this time her eyes filled with uncertainty. "I wasn't sure I was going to tell you this. I mean, on your wedding day, and all."

"There's more?" Elise was scared now. What had caused this transformation in Lavina? Was she sick? "You okay?"

Vi looked down, a little introspective. "I'm fine. Don't worry. It's just, maybe it's my age, I don't know. But I've been spending some time really thinking about what I wanted. Seeing you and Brad together has brought home the fact that time is ticking away."

"Great, another person calling me old," Elise said, trying to break the tension.

"Shut your mouth. You know what I mean. It made me take a good hard look at my relationship with Mr. G, and..."

Elise held her breath.

"And we're broken up," Lavina blurted it out. For a second, her lip wavered, and Elise thought she might cry, but she soldiered on. "I love him, I do. But, you know how I've wanted to have a family. He's had years to decide, and he just keeps putting me off. I can't keep wasting my time with someone who just doesn't want the same. I just have to move on." Lavina paused. "This is the first time I've been single since.... You know, it's embarrassing, but I can't remember when. Since before I was sixteen. Now that's sad."

"Aww, Vi." Elise reached out to hug her friend. "You're stronger than you think. You can do this on your own."

"No, Elise," Vi sniffled on her shoulder. "You've always been the strong one. You started over. You made it work. Now I'm following in your footsteps so be prepared to give me lots of advice."

"Step one," Elise grabbed her friend by the shoulders and looked her square in the eye. "No matter how messy it looks, you're going to be okay. And I always have your back. Even when you do try to get me to wear a taffeta monstrosity."

Lavina sniffled and laughed.

"Seriously! And in the winter! All I would need is a black top hat, and they'd be calling me Frosty."

"Shut your face. That dress was amazing. A real Caroline Stacy!"

"Yeah, well, thanks but no thanks." She looked fondly at her friend. "You going to be okay? With this whole wedding thing? Because you get an automatic get-out-of-maid-of-honor card. You can cash it in right now. Go chill out at the spa or something, instead."

"Elise Pepper soon to be Carter. Are you kidding me?" Lavina turned Elise around by the shoulders and pushed her out the door. "I can't even believe you'd suggest that. Now quit your dilly dallying. You have a wedding to attend."

CHAPTER 22

Oh, boy. The tears are flowing now. Elise took one look at the gazebo—at everyone's hard work at decorating it— and then at her sweet man at the end waiting for her. *I'm going to lose it. I won't even be able to see to get down the aisle.*

She sniffed and glanced at her dad. She hadn't even gotten out of the car yet. No, she wasn't going to make it.

"Aww, sweetheart," Her dad tried to gently wipe the tear rolling down her cheek. It felt more like a bear paw going after a bit of honey, but she smiled at his effort.

His forehead creased as he tried to wipe again. "I'm not doing too great, am I?" He reached into his pocket for a handkerchief. "Here you go. Don't cry. You're going to make me sad."

"You sad?" She sniffled and dabbed under her eyes. Then she smiled to show her dad that she was fine. "Why? I've already been down this road before."

"Sweetheart, that's something that I might never be able to explain to you. But seeing your daughter happy, knowing she's going to have a good life. It gets me right here." He clenched his fist and tapped his chest. "There's nothing Mom or I ever wanted in this life more than to see our daughter happy."

"I'm sorry it took me so long." She sniffled again. "I kind of made a mess of things for a while there."

He breathed out in that heavy way he always had when he was taking a moment to think. "Don't live in the past, Eli. Live in the present. Get it? Present. It's a gift. And every day you unwrap it, and you do your best with it. You take that opportunity to be grateful for something and to tell someone you love them, and you stack those presents one on top of each other knowing that you're building something worthwhile."

"And the messy mistakes?" she asked.

"The way you just looked at me reminds me of when you were a little girl." He chuckled. "You'd be coloring a picture and accidentally get out of the lines. Man, that'd make you mad. I remember taking one of those pictures and hanging it up in my office. One day, you came in and said, Daddy, why did you put that up? I messed it all up."

His warm eyes twinkled under gray brows. "You remember what I said? I said it's because it's one of a kind. It's a masterpiece. Just like you."

He reached over and hugged her. And she tried her best to quit crying.

"I love you, Eli. You ready to get out?"

She nodded then, not even able to speak. She took a few slow, deep breaths to calm herself down.

"And would you look at that." Her dad glanced up at the sky. "It's starting to snow."

Elise glanced out the window and saw it was true. Not a lot, just a few fairy flakes falling from the sky.

Her dad reached for her flowers on the seat and handed them to her. Tamara had done a beautiful job with pale peach roses, peonies and bay branches.

Her father got out and came around to her side of the car. He opened the door and helped her out. He squeezed her arm gently and smiled. A snowflake fell on her arm like an angel kiss.

Music floated through the air from the guitarist. Elise had no idea where Lavina had found him, but it was beautiful and calming.

There were more people seated there than she'd expected. Friends and family filled the white chairs that were lined up in rows before the gazebo. A length of red silk carpeted the grass walkway.

"Can everyone please stand," the Pastor directed.

Everyone's head turned in her direction. Brad caught sight of her and put his fist up to his mouth. She smiled in his direction, and he tried to smile back, but she could see he was fighting tears.

The guitarist played the wedding march, and her dad led her down the aisle. Lucy grinned from the front, while Lavina looked suspiciously puddly.

And then she was there, standing at the front, Brad staring at her like he never wanted to look away.

Her dad patted her arm. "You've got this, kiddo." He nodded to Brad, and Brad came down and took her hand.

The Pastor led them through the simple vows. Elise could still hardly speak, her voice sounding strange in her ears.

When it came time for Brad to put the ring on her finger, he hesitated, his thumb gently stroking the back of her hand.

"Elise." His voice cracked, and he cleared it. "Typical. Being around you makes me feel like a teenager sometimes."

Everyone laughed.

He smiled too, and started again. "Elise, when I first saw you in Math class all those years ago, I dreamed of this day. I don't know what clued me in, or how I knew, but in my heart, I believe then we were meant to be together. But the reality of being with you is so much better than anything I ever dreamed. I promise to love you forever, and to treat you like the gift I know I've been given." He slid the ring on her finger and kissed her hand.

Now it was Elise's turn. She'd written it out, and practiced what she'd wanted to say, but now staring into his eyes, it all flew out the window. So she went with what her heart wanted to say.

Carefully, she held his wedding band. "With this ring I promise to love you, to always stand with you, to remind you of how awesome you are on those days you forget, to help you when you fall, to protect you and fight for you when you want to give up. To share the joys of life and remind you of them on the cloudy days.

"My dad once told me when I was a little girl that I didn't need a Prince Charming. I needed a best friend and a partner, someone who would listen to me, respect me, and someone I could always respect. You are all of that, and my hero, too. I love you."

"Aww, honey. I love you, too." He brought her in to kiss her.

"Now hold up. I haven't done the official pronouncing yet," said the Pastor. He then pronounced them man and wife. "Now you can kiss your bride, young man."

Oh, boy, did Brad kiss her. Amidst the whoops and laughs the Pastor continued. "Ladies and Gentlemen, I now present to you Mr. and Mrs. Carter."

Elise was in shock as they walked back down the aisle. Because, when Brad had dipped her back and been kissing her, he'd also whispered. "And, my little bet-winner, I'm taking you to Turks and Caicos for two weeks. How's that for a honeymoon?"

At the end of the aisle, she looked into Brad's eyes and smiled. "That was just about as close to perfect as a person could ask for."

"Pretty amazing, huh? We did it," he whispered as he hugged her.

"Just one second, darlin's," came Lavina's drawl over the microphone. "On behalf of the Carters', we'd like to invite you to a reception being held at Rose Hall. Everyone know how to get there?"

People in the audience yelled back.

Lavina responded to one smart-aleck comment, "And you there, Joseph, don't be thinking...." Her voice trailed away. She stared out in the parking lot.

Elise turned to look. A black limousine was parked there, and a figure was walking toward them.

Goosebumps ran up her arms. Brad noticed and pulled her in close.

Around her, she could hear whispers.

"Is that Todd Gray, the lead singer of the Smoke and Glory country band?"

"Didn't they win the CMA's last year?"

"I know they went platinum."

"He won best male vocalist of the year three years in a row!"

The man walked firmly down the bank, sunglasses on and cowboy hat pulled low over his brow.

Elise glanced up at Lavina. She was still staring, mouth open.

"Vi!" the man called. "Vi, I need to talk with you."

The sound of her name got her moving. She put down the mic and walked briskly down the aisle.

"What are you doing here?" She glanced around at the guests.

"I can't stand it. I can't stand being without you. I'm so in love with you. Baby, we got to figure this out. I don't want to live without you. We've got to make this work. Please baby, I'm begging you. Right in front of God and all these people."

She eyed him for a second. Elise held her breath waiting to hear what Lavina would say. "All right, darlin'. Let's go talk."

Vi met Elise's gaze and winked at her as she slipped her arm through Mr. G's.

Elise watched them walk down to the shore. Maybe Elise and Brad weren't the only ones getting a happy ending today. She glanced up at Brad, not sure what to do next.

He cleared his throat. "Come on everybody! Get on down to the Rose house and help us celebrate. Drinks are on me!"

Everyone got moving with some laughter. Their family and friends surrounded them in hugs and congratulations.

It was a good day.

The End

Want a peek at the new Angel Lake series? Here is chapter

one. And keep your eyes out for a brand new series coming soon.

Booked for Murder

My name is Louisa May Marigold Swenson, Maisie for short. How in the world my parents got Maisie out of Louisa May or Marigold, I'll never know. It's my theory that my Momma wanted to name me Maisie to begin with, but with a Grandma named Louisa May, and a father whose favorite flower was of the many-petaled orange variety, she just had to sneak it in any old way she could.

Momma has called me Maisie for all of my life, only trotting out my full name when calling me home for dinner, or when she'd discovered the cookie jar was empty, or the dog had been given a haircut—although to be fair, I was five at the time. Still, I can hear her voice ring out over the air, especially at twilight on a summer's eve.

And not just because it's a childhood memory. No, Momma lives with me, along with her basset hound, Bingo. That dog is something else. The story that Momma tried to spin was that she got him for my birthday—my thirty-fourth birthday, mind you. Momma expected me to go ga-ga over the floppy-eared pup like I was still in pigtails unwrapping gifts under the Christmas tree.

Well, I did go ga-ga. I can't lie. Who could resist a basset hound puppy with those giant crocodile feet to match dark brown eyes?

Bingo adores me. I'd love to say that's unique but, truth be told, he adores anyone with food. I've always said he'd betray our whole family for a French fry, which makes Momma frown. Although he loves all people, the dog is especially bonded to Momma, I think half because she's always here with him and the other half because she keeps a box of Nabisco vanilla wafers nearby that she insists are to aid with her digestion. Kind of supports my theory, because I have a good feeling they help Bingo's digestion pretty well, too.

I'm originally from Angel Lake, a gorgeous little town in Tennessee, but I recently scored my dream job down here in Starke Springs, Florida as a manager at the Oceanside Hotel, complete with a complimentary suite on the bottom floor. It's only two blocks from the beach and near the most amazing amusement park. Not the iconic one with ear hats. We have a squirrel on ours. That's just our thing, and we do treasure it.

Technically, I applied for the hotel manager's job and moved down here from Tennessee to look after Momma. I wouldn't tell her that, though. She's apt to pull out a darning needle and threaten to chase me with it. Not that she could chase very far, but I'd rather not get her riled up.

Momma believes I moved here for the job, and because I'm

desperate for her help in finding a man. "Maisie, you keep going like you are, and you're going to be living in Spinsterville," she likes to warn me. Her not-so-subtle hints let me know she secretly feels like she's my last hope to find me a good match, and actually believes she's the one taking care of me.

Truth be told, I haven't been having a lot of luck in the man department, so I can use all the help I can get. Or not get. Some days, I am completely okay with living the single life. Other days are so lonely even Bingo's sad eyes can't capture what I feel inside.

Anyhow, they say the strangest things happen in hotels, and I'm here to say they're right. Let me tell you what happened when we had only been living at the Oceanside Hotel for two weeks. It started like this.

———

IT WAS LUNCHTIME, and I headed home to the suite. My stomach made a loud unladylike noise, picturing the meal Momma had prepared. She could cook the meanest roast beef, butternut squash, and French-cut green beans that you've ever seen. That was one of the many good things about moving in together.

Opening the door, I took a big sniff. Immediately, I started coughing. *What the heck was that smell?* A cross between hellfire and burnt broccoli.

"Momma?" I yelled, slightly horrified to see smoke hanging in thick swirls near the ceiling. I rushed through the suite and opened the sliding glass door. Spotting a towel, I grabbed it and started waving. "Momma? Where are you? Are you okay?"

First to greet me was Bingo, the Basset. He meandered over, tongue lolling and tail wagging.

Momma walked in next, shuffling in slippers and a pink housecoat and carrying a bag of microwaved popcorn. Her hair was a brassy red—she called it strawberry blonde—and came from the salon down the street by a hairdresser named Genessa. Momma liked to say that Genessa was a far better listener than her own daughter and would make her a grandma before I do. I never knew what Momma was saying with that statement; was she threatening to adopt Genessa and replace me? Or was it just digging at the fact that I didn't have a husband or even a prospect on the horizon yet?

Momma grabbed a handful of popcorn from the bag and put a kernel in her mouth. Half the bag sported black scorch marks.

"What on earth is going on here?" I started out slow, still waving my towel.

"I made myself a snack to eat while I watch my stories."

Stories was what Momma called her soaps since I was a little girl. There was a wide-eyed innocent look in her eye. I didn't fall for it.

"You're just eating popcorn? I thought you were making lunch?" My stomach rumbled to underline that thought.

"Darlin', I'm on a diet. Swimsuit season is coming up in just a few more weeks." She shuffled back into the living room with her charred bag.

Bingo quickly passed me when he realized the food had left the room. *How can she eat that?* I followed them, confused.

"Why on earth is the popcorn bag black on one side?" I asked, almost scared to hear the answer.

"I saw this lovely craft on Pinterest I was going to make for the hotel convention tomorrow. Earn me some pocket money. But something's wrong with your microwave," she answered with a dismissive wave. She popped another piece into her mouth, her eyes glued to the TV set.

Inwardly, I groaned as I headed back into the kitchen. Visions of a plate of roast beef, gravy and potatoes disappeared before my eyes as I saw the disaster awaiting me. *What on earth has she done?*

Dirty measuring cups and bowls towered in the sink. I felt

something crunch under my foot and glanced to see sugar sprinkled about like deranged fairy-dust. On the counter were two empty bottles of Elmer's Glue, bits of leaves and flowers, and one of her recipe cards. I picked it up and read the recipe, smiling a bit at the smudged fingerprint.

Homemade Fake-Acrylic Pendants.

Looking farther down the counter, there were several used spoons, three dirty towels, and a frying pan. I had to admit, the pan alarmed me. What did a pan have to do with necklace pendants?

First things first. I shook my head and mentally girded my loins as I opened the microwave. Still, as prepared as I was, I gasped.

Baked-on streaks and splatters covered the interior. I covered my eyes, trying to figure out what she could have done to have caused this mess. How long had she melted the glue? To lava temperatures? I peeked through my hand. *And then she microwaved the popcorn on the mess left behind.*

I was more than a little worried. Momma was a character, but she generally didn't do things this nutty. I grabbed my cell and quickly dialed my closest friend in the area, Ruby.

I'd met Ruby in junior high, during those awkward years when braces and zits defined me. She'd traveled from Florida to Tennessee that year for a summer camp, and we'd hit it right off. We'd joined the camp's fast-pitch team and played baseball with the other camps in the area. The next few summers we continued to meet up. Even in high school, we managed to work together as camp counselors. And, I have to admit, I became a champion pitcher.

Ruby answered on the third ring. "Hey, lady. What's cooking?"

"Funny you should ask," I reached for a sponge to scrub out the microwave. "Right now, I'm cleaning Momma's attempt at making diamonds in the microwave."

Ruby clucked her tongue. "That bad, huh? What was she doing?"

"I think she may have had it in mind that she would be the great bling proprietor for the Comic Convention tomorrow."

"Oh, that's funny. You should have taken her up on it." Then, hearing my frustrated huff, she quickly changed the subject. "Have you ever overseen anything like a Comic-Con before? Are you nervous?"

"No, and no." My phone vibrated softly, alerting me to a message. "Hey, I better get going. I'll talk to you later."

"You better believe it! I want to hear all about it!"

I pushed the end button and squinted to see the text on the screen.

Inside the little green bubble were the words—*What are you wearing?*

A groan wrenched out of me. The text came from my boss, the owner of the Oceanside Hotel, Mr. Timothy Phillips. Despite the dubious wording, he was asking if I was planning to wear a costume to the convention tomorrow.

My answer was—*Not a costume.*

I rolled my eyes and walked into my room. There was my dress suit, pressed and hanging in the closet. I sure hoped tomorrow wouldn't be too weird.

The Sweet Taste of Murder

UNTITLED

Made in the USA
Monee, IL
05 November 2020